DIS(

AN OPEN HEART

CAROLINE WARFIELD

Cover design by Claudia Bost at CWB Designs

This story first appeared in *Holly and Hopeful Hearts*, the 2016 box set of the Bluestocking Belles. Each of us used characters belonging to other authors in our stories. The participating authors have given me license to publish this story as a stand-alone with their characters included. I give special thanks to Jude Knight for the Belvoir, Grenford, and Winderfield families, and her lovely duchess.

DEDICATION

For my grandson, may he always value tradition

CHAPTER 1

A young lady stepped out of her father's carriage into the sunshine of Great St. Helen's Street in Bishopsgate, looked up at a cloudless sky, and controlled the urge to dance with great difficulty. She clutched a cream-colored missive in one hand and her skirt in the other as if to tread a few steps, but dancing would not be seemly behavior. Even though the song in her heart sent music all the way to her toes, Esther refrained, but she couldn't control the smile that spread across her face.

Her maid and ever-present companion, Reba, lumbered down behind her. "Miss Esther, you look fit to explode. Remember your mother's words."

"'Ladies do not run. Ladies do not skip. Ladies walk with grace and…' Oh, please, Reba. I know it by heart. Today you can't dampen my joy."

For once she cared not a whit that her family home, elegant and sumptuous though it may be, lay inside the city walls and close to commercial enterprises. An actual duchess had given her—Esther Baumann, banker's daughter—an invitation to a country house party that would culminate in a ball. Her Grace handed it to her personally, and a warm smile went with it. Mama might fret, but she believed Papa would allow her to accept. She would not only visit Hollystone Hall but also dance at a ball. Her day seemed almost too perfect to be true.

Esther skipped up the steps to the massive front door with Reba scurrying behind her muttering warnings.

"Good afternoon, Smithers. Isn't it a lovely afternoon?" she chirped to the butler as she swished by him. "Where is my father?"

She didn't wait for an answer. This time of day, Papa would be home and he would be in his study. She strode down the hall without heeding the butler's, "Miss Esther, you might not want—"

Silence met her when she swept into the study. Papa was not alone, and his frown boded ill. Esther stood rooted to the spot, momentarily speechless.

Two gentlemen surged to their feet immediately. The tallest, with hair so blond it appeared white in the afternoon shadows, looked down his aristocratic nose with ice blue eyes and made a perfectly correct bow. She knew the Marquess of Glenaire on sight. His sister, a horrid girl, had been at school with Esther, albeit a few years younger. The other gentleman appeared to be Glenaire's equal in class, breeding, and refinement, and yet he looked at her with kind eyes the color of warm coffee. She believed he fought to contain a smile. Esther let out the breath she held, smiled back, and curtseyed politely.

Behind the two of them, a third man rose, and Esther's smile fled. This one she knew well. Her heart gave a stutter as it always did at the sight of Adam Halevy, her father's protégée. She devoutly wished it did not. His coal black hair, magnificent form, and piercing eyes never failed to affect her. Usually, they left her breathless. Today, those eyes were neither icy, nor warm. They looked furious. "Miss Baumann," he said through clenched teeth with the slightest bow. "This is unexpected."

A shift of her shoulder cut Adam and his disapproving frown from her line of sight. "I apologize, Papa. I didn't know you had company. I'll leave you gentlemen to your business."

Her father rose to his feet, and Esther felt the surge of pride she often did. In his mid-forties, Baumann radiated intelligence and power. Even his genial manner, and the habitual twinkle in his eyes, didn't disguise the single-minded intensity with which he had built his business. Straight as an arrow and only slightly silver at the temples, Nathaniel Baumann had become in maturity every inch an English gentleman. His boyhood in a German ghetto disappeared behind his English looks and voice, and, more so, behind his very real dedication to his adopted country.

"Gentleman, I believe our business is complete. Allow me to present my daughter, Miss Esther Baumann. Esther, may I present the Marquess of Glenaire and Viscount Rochlin. You know Mr. Halevy, of course."

Esther demonstrated her perfectly correct curtsey to the gentlemen. "I'm honored, my lords," she murmured while curiosity raged through her.

The two gentlemen made polite responses and began to take their leave.

"I think your daughter has a message of some importance for you, Baumann," Viscount Rochlin said, nodding at the folded vellum in Esther's hand with a smile.

Papa sighed. "It would appear so. What is so important that you had to interrupt my meeting, daughter?" He held out his hand.

Mortification sent heat up Esther's neck. Suddenly, she

wanted to hug the invitation to herself, but all four men looked at her expectantly, so she handed it over meekly.

When her father unfolded the heavy vellum everyone in the study could see that it was a formally printed notice of some sort. "An invitation, Esther?" he murmured.

"Yes, Papa. The Duchess of Haverford gave it to me personally," she replied.

"The Charity Ball," Glenaire observed flatly. "Her Grace is not taking no for an answer on that one. " He looked at Viscount Rochlin. "You'll have a lucky escape at least. The matchmaking mamas are already on the hunt."

Rochlin waved the teasing away. "I'd rather be back in the saddle in the Pyrenees than in dancing slippers, even at a Haverford ball."

"Then you best get packed, Will, if you and Halevy plan to leave today," Glenaire said to his friend, shocking Esther with his use of the man's first name.

In a matter of moments, the men had retrieved their hats, made their polite goodbyes, and left, Esther stood in the elegant foyer between her father and Adam, who glowered at her under lowered brows, mystified by the gentlemen's presence and the meeting she had interrupted.

Esther ignored Adam and looked at her father with so many questions she didn't know where to start.

Baumann tapped the invitation against the palm of one hand. "Interesting event. I'll discuss it with your mother," he said pointedly.

"I thought you would be pleased!"

"With the Haverford connection? Of course, but this is a country house party. I can't leave London, and your mother is too weak to travel."

"I have Reba," Esther said, heart sinking. She knew a maid would not be a sufficient chaperone. A quick glance at Adam confirmed his disapproval of that idea.

"Perhaps your Aunt Dinah . . . " He shrugged. "See Adam out, would you?" he asked with a twinkle. He started up the stairs toward her mother's sitting room and left her alone with the one person who both attracted and infuriated her.

"Why are you leaving? Why did the viscount mention the Pyrenees?" she demanded, as much to forestall any comments about her plans to attend the duchess's ball as to satisfy her roiling curiosity.

"Your father is sending gold to Wellington." Adam replied, running a hand across the back of his neck. "The government is temporarily unable to fund their war in Spain."

She rose on the balls of her feet. "Papa can arrange this?" Pride and excitement pushed other emotions away.

"With the help of his contacts in France, yes. We're taking it across the Pyrenees."

Esther knew better than to ask how they would arrange it. Cousins across Europe would be involved. One thought overrode all others.

"It will be dangerous."

He looked for a moment as if he wouldn't answer. His face when he did touched her heart. "Probably, but the viscount and I will watch out for each other. You aren't to worry about me, Esther."

At the use of her name, Esther smiled. She ought to correct him for presuming, but in truth, it pleased her. For a moment, they looked at each other in perfect harmony.

"Be careful," she whispered.

"I will."

The moment grew awkward, and Esther thought she should say something. "You're going to safeguard Papa's interests?" she asked.

He nodded. "And the viscount will safeguard England's."

"They don't trust you because you're French."

"They don't trust me because I'm Jewish," he replied bitterly.

"Viscount Rochlin looked friendly enough."

"Looks can deceive, Miss Baumann. You shouldn't trust them either. Your father should not be encouraging your association with these aristocrats."

"Why ever not? The duchess is kindness itself, and a number of my schoolmates will be there. It is my first ball and—"

"—I don't understand how your father could send you to that school. Your parents are entirely too secular in their outlook. The Talmud suggests—"

"I wouldn't know what your precious books suggest. I'm excluded from that kind of learning." There. She had given voice to her greatest resentment. Let him make what he would out of that.

"Your Mother—"

"Leave my mother out of this. My mother taught me what I need to know about Shabbat and the holy days. And who are you to criticize?"

Adam colored, red blotches staining his cheeks. "Of course I have no right. I had hoped before I left—"

Esther felt light-headed for a moment. Had he spoken to Papa? Breath rushed back into her lungs, but she raised her chin. "What is it you hoped, Mr. Halevy?"

Adam's eyes softened, and Ether found herself leaning slightly toward him. A moment later, he stiffened and took a step back.

"My wife will respect our traditions and keep a traditional home," he announced.

"I wish you luck finding such a paragon, Mr. Halevy," Esther responded, pulling herself up as tall as she could. "My home will respect tradition and the people we meet." When he simply glared at her outburst, she went on, "And my daughters will know as much about our faith as you do!"

"Good luck to you in that endeavor, Miss Bauman," he said with a jerky nod. He tapped his hat on his head with more force than needed.

When he stepped out the door, Esther couldn't control the urge to dart out after him. "Adam—Mr. Halevy—wait!"

His frown looked more puzzled than angry when he turned to her.

"Where you're going—it will be dangerous." Her lack of breath made the words sound uneven.

Adam nodded.

"I—" The expression on his face stopped her before she could continue. "I'll pray for you," she finished at last, "and the success of your journey, of course."

A sad smile transformed his face. "I would be grateful for your prayers, Miss Baumann."

She watched him walk down the street, biting down on her lower lip to hold back tears.

CHAPTER 2

I*'ll pray for you.*

The words followed Adam to the coast, across the Channel to a secluded cove on the French homeland until they became a sort of talisman, as if his safety depended on Esther Baumann far away in England.

He stepped onto a pebble-strewn beach behind Viscount Rochlin. The vessel that brought them, the marquess's private yacht, had been luxurious beyond Adam's experience, even among his wealthy relatives. "Trust Richard," Rochlin had said, "To send us into Hell in style." The viscount seemed more amused than impressed. Adam had to admit every effort had been made to see to his comfort. Once they landed, however, they were on their own, and arrangements were up to Adam.

By the time they rested in Abram Baumann's house in Paris and began their trip south, he had to admit Rochlin was agreeable company. The viscount rested amiably enough in a Jewish banker's house; he made only practical suggestions regarding the use of a false-bottomed and battered old carriage to hide gold; he found the plan that included his role as "Monsieur Delacroix's" deaf mute cousin amusing. Still, the man was heir to the Earl of Chadbourn, and, if gossip proved correct, soon to inherit. People like that put their personal interests first. Adam viewed him with great caution.

The two men rode side by side in front of the carriage, matching their pace to the lumbering vehicle's maddening slowness. On the road between towns, the viscount could at least speak. Their driver, loyal to Abram Baumann, kept his own council.

"Next time, don't forget to imply I am deaf as well as mute," the viscount remarked on the third afternoon. "It will loosen tongues when I'm around."

That made sense. Adam had realized very quickly that, terrible though his accent may be, Rochlin understood French perfectly well. He listened and missed nothing.

"As you wish, my lord."

Rochlin rolled his eyes. "That's another thing. You call me Guillaume in front of others. Call me Will when we're alone. You'll drive me mad my-lording me."

"Correct etiquette demands—"

"Etiquette be damned. I've seen more than one mission go awry because some officer with more lace than brains demanded his due at the expense of the objective. We are partners in this enterprise. It would help if you could treat me accordingly, whether others are present or not."

Adam wondered if he meant it, truly. While his statement made some practical sense, Adam doubted it would extend to viewing a Jew as his equal under any other circumstances. He didn't respond.

"Stubborn man," Rochlin mumbled under his breath.

Neither man spoke for the next two hours. An inn came into view midafternoon.

"It's too early to stop," Rochlin said.

Adam stared at a map and strained his memory. At the

pace of the carriage, their journey would take them five hours to reach the next town. "If we press ahead we'll reach the next posting inn well after dark. I don't see how we can do it."

"We could camp tonight," Rochlin suggested. "Are you up for sleeping on the ground?"

The suggestion startled Adam. He had lived simply enough as a student in Mont-Ombre, but he'd never been an outdoorsman and certainly didn't expect it of a viscount.

"Come, come, man. I spent four years fighting the French in the Peninsula. I've slept under stars more nights than not. You can have the carriage if you prefer."

Adam bristled at the implication he was less of a man than the viscount. "I can sleep out if we must."

"We must. This pace is killing me. This was to be my first Yuletide home after years of war. I want to get back. Don't you?"

"For Christmas?" Adam demanded, swallowing bile.

"No, you daft man. I know your tradition is otherwise. I meant to family, to friends… to Miss Baumann." He shot Adam a sly smile.

Adam found himself smiling back. "You wish to spend your holidays with your family?" he asked.

"Family is everything. You could join us. You might like Chadbourn Hall filled with greenery, plum pudding, and song." The viscount shrugged. "Or you might want to hurry to London once we return. Isn't your family there?"

"My parents are dead," Adam told him. "Mr. Baumann is a cousin, rather distant unfortunately."

"No family? I can't imagine anything worse," Rochlin said sadly.

Adam remembered belatedly that the dying earl wasn't just a title. This man's father lay ill. No wonder he wanted to get home as soon as possible.

"If we could lighten the carriage, we might go faster. We've already removed ourselves and what baggage we can fasten to our horses," he suggested.

"What if we put the baggage back into the carriage and removed some of its heavier load?" Rochlin asked.

"The gold?"

Rochlin nodded. "We can sew it into our saddles and into our shirts. We can't take it all, but removing even some of the weight should help. Our exploring officers used clever pockets to carry sensitive messages and, yes, gold. We'll need some fustian and needles, but it can be done."

"You sew?" Adam laughed.

"I sew. I cook. I am a man of many talents. War teaches many things. Do you think this town big enough to have a draper's shop?"

"No, but the next one will."

"So tonight we sleep under the stars, and tomorrow we shop." Rochlin grinned.

"As you wish, my lord," Adam said sarcastically.

Rochlin made sound that imitated a dog's growl.

Adam laughed. "If you insist. It may just work—Will."

They bedded down in a farmer's field that night. Adam paid the man a few sou, so he gave them straw for bedding. Will, as Adam now tried to think of him, declined. "Straw breeds bugs," he whispered when they were out of earshot.

Adam lay on the hard ground, wrapped in a blanket and his greatcoat, and stared up at a moonless sky strewn with stars. Did Esther Baumann look out on the same stars? Even in London, the brighter ones would be visible. The memory of her voice came to him then. *I'll pray for you*, he heard, and he fell asleep.

CHAPTER 3

"Speak respectfully to your mother." Habitual affection softened Nathaniel Baumann's stern command, even as he gave his daughter a pointed look.

"Sorry, Mama," Esther murmured. "I just don't understand why you object."

Miriam Baumann lay under shawls on her settee; her pallor and shaking hands gave testimony to chronic illness. Her frown seemed to imply she found Esther willful and wanting, and Esther wondered if her mother ever understood her. She bit her lip in anticipation of a scold. A long sigh preceded her mama's reply. "These balls. The upper classes use them to marry their daughters to rich and titled gentlemen. There is no place for you in that world, Esther."

It was on the tip of Esther's tongue to demand to know why not, but her father's concerned glance from where he loomed over her mother's sickbed stopped her. She clutched the satin covering on both arms of the plush side chair in which she sat and chose her words carefully. "It won't be that kind of ball, Mama. The entire event has been arranged for the duchess's charity. The money will go to fund schools, especially for girls."

"English girls," Mama said bitterly.

"Surely those English girls need all the education we can support," Papa said with a twinkle in his eye.

His support strengthened Esther's determination. "All girls need it. The sort of schools the duchess supports will teach more than needlework and dancing," she replied.

"I thought you liked that school we sent you to." Mama sighed.

"I did, mostly. My French is much improved, and the library offered interest. Those schools could be so much better."

"And you made friends with some of the best families," Papa said proudly.

Esther smiled back at him. He valued business contacts, but she knew he genuinely wanted her to find a place among the powerful families for her own sake.

"I did. Felicity Belvoir and her sister Sophia will be at the house party. I long to join them."

"Out of the question," her mother said. "I've heard about those house parties."

"There won't be scandal, Mama, I'm sure of it. The duchess will host it personally, and she will see to it the behavior is all that is proper."

Mama looked skeptical. "Perhaps if I could take you, yes, but you must know that is impossible."

Esther turned toward her father, hope lodged in her chest.

He shook his head sadly. "I can't leave town. Business keeps me here. I'll send a large contribution with our regrets."

"You see? The Baumanns will do their part for your cause.

There is no reason for you to go. You will not meet your future husband there, Esther."

Why can't I marry a titled gentleman? Her face crumpled into a frown, but then Adam Halevy's handsome face popped into memory. The infuriating man turned her insides to jelly, even though his highhanded ways put a wedge between them. Why couldn't she look elsewhere? The Marquess of Glenaire and his friend seemed amiable enough. Felicity Belvoir's brother, the Earl of Hythe, had been very polite on his visits to the school. The thought of his dashing appearance made her shiver. All three handsome titled men had made her smile. There would be others. *Why shouldn't I at least dance, flirt, and enjoy their company?* Resentment made her as unhappy as could be.

Mama went on without noticing Esther's preoccupation. "The matchmaker will find a perfect husband in the community for you, Esther, as is traditional. This party is not your world."

"But, Papa," Esther burst out, ignoring her mother. "It would be rude to refuse the Duchess of Haverford's invitation. Her support could be valuable, couldn't it?"

Papa looked thoughtful.

Another idea came to her. "I may be able to persuade her to include Jewish schools in her charity. Aren't Montefiore and the others planning a Jewish Free School for London?"

"For boys, yes," Papa said.

"Why not girls as well? I want more for my daughters." Esther colored at that. "That is, when I have them."

Papa nodded sagely. "We need well educated mothers for our children," he said.

"I want them to know the Talmud as well as Adam Halevy knows it," Esther told them.

Her mother's laugh came harsh and fast. "Mr. Halevy

studied with the rabbis for four years. He is a respected scholar. You can't expect—"

"Why not?" Esther demanded.

"It isn't a woman's place," Mama said, as if that settled the matter.

Esther stiffened and bit her lip to hold back her reply.

Papa's raised brows communicated more than words. Not now. Not here.

"What about Dinah?" he asked after an awkward silence.

"What about her?" Mama asked.

"Dinah could escort Esther to Hollystone Hall."

"Nathaniel, your sister doesn't budge from our parlor or bestir herself unless you tell her to," Mama said bitterly.

Esther knew she had the right of it. She dreaded the thought of traveling in her aunt's close company. Still, if it meant she could go to the house party and ball… "She will do it for you, Papa, if you ask her," Esther told her father hopefully. *At least if you order her to.*

"Miriam?" he asked.

Mama sunk back against her pillows. "There is no dissuading your daughter, Nathaniel. Do what you think is best."

Papa beamed at Esther, and her heart soared.

"I'll respond to the invitation on the family's behalf, Esther. Perhaps you might send a more personal note to Her Grace?"

Esther surged to her feet and prepared to bolt off.

"Use your best handwriting, Esther, and be sure to use correct address. And Esther," Mama called. "Ladies do not run."

CHAPTER 4

The road began to rise at last into the towering Pyrenees. Six weeks after leaving London, after hard and often tedious travel, they crawled into the village of Mont-Ombre in the lower reaches of the mountains. Tonight, at least, Adam would sleep among friends. If the viscount objected, he would have to suffer in silence.

Adam led his companion to a sturdy stone house on the edge of the village. Two rows of windows ranged across each of its flat sides, and painted flower boxes, empty now in the late autumn gloom, hung beneath each window. Children playing in the front garden scattered at their approach, alerting their elders to the visitors. An old man appeared in the doorway. His grizzled hair curled around a brimless hat, and a long robe, open at the front, covered a plain shirt and trousers.

"Adam! Son of my heart, welcome."

Adam leaned forward in his saddle and greeted the old man. "Honored teacher, blessings on your house."

"And on yours. We expected you three days ago. I had begun to worry."

"It could not be helped. Our burdens are heavy, Rabbi." Adam glanced back at the carriage. He dismounted, and the viscount followed suit.

"They're expecting us?" Will whispered.

"Most certainly. They are a crucial part of our journey," Adam whispered back. Raising his voice, he made introductions. "Viscount Rochlin, may I present Rebbe Benyamin Nahmany, the finest Talmudic scholar in Europe."

The old man bowed deeply. "The honor is mine, my lord. My young friend exaggerates."

Will returned the bow with a charming smile. "I have never known Mr. Halevy to exaggerate, sir."

"Ah, good to hear. Perhaps my teaching was not in vain," the old man replied with a wink. "Come, come, my Alma will already be cooking, delighted to have two more hardy young men to devour her masterpieces."

"The carriage—" Will began.

"My sons will care for it," Rebbe Nahmany said.

Adam answered Will's unspoken question. "We can trust this family with our lives." To his teacher, he asked, "Mikal and Dan?"

"Mikal is married and giving me grandchildren! Dan will help Yakov do it. We have three students this year. They also may be of assistance."

"Come inside, Will, and I'll explain."

Will watched over his shoulder as three young men, one no more than a boy, led the horses and carriages away and an army of children carried their personal baggage into the house and up a narrow stairway. Within moments, they were seated in deep cushions before a friendly fire, and a young woman bustled to serve them fragrant tea in colorful cups.

"Greetings, Beth," Adam guessed.

The old man laughed. "You have been gone too long. Beth is long married. This is my Sarah."

"My apologies, Sarah. The last time I saw you, you ran barefoot down the road to say goodbye, pigtails flying. You must have been—what—eight?"

"Nine, Mr. Halevy." The young woman looked at Adam under dark lashes and blushed deeply.

"It is rude of you to remind this lovely young woman of that, Adam," Will said, smiling at the girl. "My sisters would never forgive me if I spoke thus in front of stranger."

Sarah colored more deeply and scurried back to the kitchen. Adam watched Will closely but saw no sign of improper interest in the girl. His suspicious mind shamed him.

"I think I had better explain what happens next," he said to turn the subject, and he began to outline what Nathaniel Baumann and his European cousins had arranged. The gold would be unloaded here. Adam, Will, and the Nahmany sons would carry it into the mountains using three farm carts and oxen, all of them disguised as farm laborers.

"The carriage would never make it up those hills. Your 'Guillaume' will have to go a bit farther I fear." Adam looked at Will cautiously.

"No problem there. I know these mountains. How far can the farm carts go?" The viscount leaned forward, elbows on knees.

"As far as they need to. A troop of soldiers will meet us led by Major James Heyworth. Do you know him?"

"Jamie?" A grin split the Will's face. "I know him very well. Our escort?"

Adam nodded. "They will bring horses. We'll transfer the cargo to a dozen horses, split into two groups, and approach Wellington's headquarters via back roads or no roads at all from two directions to lessen the risk."

"I assume he is still at Freineda." Will looked over at the rabbi.

Rebbe Nahmany shrugged and held his hands wide. "Or Cuidad Rodrigo. The troops will know."

Will nodded deep in thought. "Jamie will see to it," he murmured.

"You wish you were on the other side of this transaction," Adam said. He didn't form it as a question.

The viscount nodded sadly and attempted a smile. "Hooky ordered me home at my father's request when his illness worsened. My life isn't mine to order."

The realization that a man born to a privilege could have even less freedom than he did surprised Adam. Once again, sympathy for his traveling companion overran old preconceptions.

The viscount must have seen it in Adam's face. "I'm needed, Adam. Family first. I admit I'm glad for this interlude, but it will be over for me again soon enough. You might have told me all this sooner, though."

"I assumed your friend the marquess told you. The last part involving the troops was his doing."

Will shook his head. "He didn't say a word. Typical. Richard likes to arrange our lives."

Rebbe Nahmany looked from one to the other. "That is settled then?"

Both young men nodded.

"Let us talk of other things, then, although perhaps equally as unfortunate. I must extend sympathy, Adam. Word reached us that your parents died soon after you reached England. One right after the other."

"My mother nursed him as long as she could before succumbing to the fever herself. They sent me to Allya's house to keep me away." Old familiar tears welled. "I wasn't there."

"Your sister is well settled?" the old teacher asked.

"My parents arranged a good match for her with a physician in York. She is well."

"But far, I think, leaving you without family." The old man shook his head.

"Tragic for you," Will murmured. The viscount looked lost in thought.

Adam smiled his gratitude but didn't voice it.

He started to reply to Rebbe Nahmany that Nathaniel Baumann, distant though their kinship was, treated him well, but thoughts of the viscount's troubles distracted him. "We will get you back for your holidays, Will. You have my word to do my best."

The viscount's mouth quirked. "And we'll get you to your Miss Baumann."

"She isn't—" Adam felt his face heat. When he didn't finish the sentence, the viscount chuckled.

A pleasant hour passed while Adam and his former teacher caught up on shared acquaintances. Adam glanced at his traveling companion several times, wondering how he reacted to this old Jewish teacher and stories of his seven children and many grandchildren. Each time, the viscount seemed genuinely interested. When Will topped one of the rabbi's stories of a mischievous grandson with one of his own, they all laughed, and Adam relaxed.

Alma Nahmany called them into dinner. That's when he noticed the menorah. Hanukah! He had forgotten about it in the midst of travel and worry. How many days had passed? He watched the old woman light five candles, smiling at her husband. His weary brain tried to calculate the date and failed. Somewhere in the last week or so of November.

After the blessing, they pulled out chairs, and the viscount leaned over to whisper, "You needn't look at me as if I'm going to turn into a society beau. Family is family. I'm not that different."

Will began to regale the young ones with stories that kept them laughing, and Adam felt a fool. A raised eyebrow and knowing look from Rebbe Nahmany didn't help the growing realization that he had judged the viscount with prejudice.

Toward the end of the meal, one of Rebbe Nahmany's students glanced at the old man slyly and turned to Sarah. "Have you managed to translate that passage from Bereishith?" he asked her.

The girl blushed furiously.

Her father rebuked him, "Don't tease the girl, Avram. She knew the Hebrew well enough and your meaning also. If you wish to talk of marriage, talk with her mother."

Sarah dropped her head to her hands while the entire table laughed. She began to clear dishes. "There is cake," she said, "If my brothers can stop laughing long enough."

At the viscount's puzzled expression, Adam explained, "The book is 'Beginning.' You would call it Genesis. He probably alluded to the quote, 'for this a man shall leave his father and his mother…' Marriage."

The young man grinned at that.

"She reads it in Hebrew?" Will asked. "I'm impressed."

Impressed. Can Esther Baumann read Hebrew?

"Aren't we all?" One of her brothers guffawed, setting off another round of laughter.

"You need not look so amazed, Adam Halevy," Rebbe Nahmany said. "All my daughters read the Torah, but Sarah is particularly adept. Does not the Devarim compel us to teach our children the law? Who better to teach the children than their mothers?"

"Deuteronomy, yes, but the Talmud at least is forbidden," Adam said, helping himself to potatoes while struggling to keep his worldview from tilting on its axis. Doubt that began when he quarreled with Esther grew daily.

The rabbi shrugged. "The Talmud and the oral traditions

are complex. Few women wish to dedicate their lives to their study. The sage Ben-Azzai suggested fathers should teach their daughters sufficient Talmud to—"

"But, Rabbi, Eliezer—"

"Yes, yes, we all know what Eliezer taught. The man did not like women." Rebbe Nahmany chuckled. "How can my daughters value our faith if they do not know it, I ask you?"

How indeed?

Cake arrived, and the conversation shifted. The education of women lost ground to ribald teasing, popular literature, and the emperor's disastrous invasion of Russia. Nahmany, like many Jews, supported Napoleon initially. As reform morphed into new tyranny, the emperor's government pulled back earlier decrees on religious freedom. When the emperor's grandiose ambitions led a generation of young men to war across Europe, and anti-Semitism reared its head in parts of France, Nahmany's support for him evaporated. The Corsican needed to be stopped for France's sake.

Late that night, Adam stared at the rafters of the attic, and the rabbi's words returned to haunt him. Who would be his children's first teacher? Their mother.

Esther Baumann would make a wonderful first teacher. Her final words in London stayed with him while he drifted off to sleep and smiled in his dreams. *I'll pray for you, Adam Halevy.*

CHAPTER 5

They left the next morning as six poor laborers driving three farm wagons pulled by oxen and loaded with hay and livestock. If stopped, they could say they carried provisions for whichever army stopped them. It seemed a good plan.

Rebbe Nahmany rose at dawn to see them off and offer his blessing. "Son of my heart, will I see you when you return?"

Adam accepted the old man's embrace. "God willing, but I can't promise we'll pass this way." Once into the hills, things could change rapidly.

"Go then, Adam, but if I don't see you again, remember these words from a man who has lived long: keep an open heart."

Keep an open heart. During the long slow climb, Adam had ample time to ponder the rabbi's meaning. He rode in the middle of the three wagons, while Viscount Rochlin—Will—rode on the lead wagon with muskets that lay hidden under a thin layer of straw within reach. He had certainly misjudged the man who had been nothing but friendly and tolerant the entire trip. *Open mind or open heart? Have I closed mine?* Did the old rabbi suspect his quarrel with Esther?

The wagon lurched, drawing his attention back to the job at hand, and he prayed they wouldn't need those muskets.

For two days, their journey toward Wellington's head-quarters went as planned. On the third day, they woke to icy rains and hellish roads. Progress slowed to a crawl. At the top of a rise, the third wagon slipped into deep mire and stuck.

The men pulled the two lead wagons forward to a level part of the road and came back to help. Will pulled out two muskets. "Which of you can fire this?"

Dan Nahmany raised a hand. "I'm a deft hand with rabbits," he said.

Tossing one of the muskets to the young man, the viscount scanned the clearing. "Good. Frenchmen are slower than rabbits." He stopped abruptly. Every man there, Jew or not, was French. "Sorry. Let's say the emperor's unfortunate followers are slower. We're sitting ducks out here in the open."

Avram, Sarah's erstwhile suitor who had been driving the third wagon, began to dig around the axils of the mired wagon.

Adam looked downhill at the work and back at his part-ner. "Won't the guns make it obvious we aren't poor farm-ers?" he asked.

"If a patrol sees us, they may not ask what nationality we are," Will said. "We can continue to be poor farmers, but I'll feel better if one or two of us are hidden up that hill with the muskets." He looked at Adam as if considering something. "Can you shoot?" he asked at last.

"I can shoot," Adam told him ruefully. "Probably better than I can shift wagons."

"I've moved my share of buried axels. You take Dan up

and hide in those rocks, and I'll help Avram and the others. " He stripped off his jacket without hesitation. "If a patrol approaches, stay down unless they appear to threaten us. If they do, shoot them."

From his perch atop a boulder, Adam watched the viscount work, skill and experience evidenced in every movement. He found it hard to match the fashionable lord he met in Baumann's study with the sweating muscular man laboring beside Nahmany's students as they dug, levered boards under wheels, and urged oxen forward. Finally, on the last try, the wagon rolled forward. As quickly as it did, it slid back with force.

A shriek brought Adam and Dan to their feet.

"Avram!" Will shouted. The scholarly young man had been pushing from behind.

By the time Adam scrambled down the hill, the viscount was on his knees in the mud next to the young man. "Everyone push!" he shouted. The wagon gave, and Will pulled Avram clear before the wagon sank back.

They ordered Dan back up the hill, but Adam stayed.

"The rest of you begin unloading that damned wagon," Will said, his attention on the white face of the injured man. "Sorry, Adam. We should have unloaded before," he said under his breath. His hands probed for injury. "His ribs feel fine, but that leg is badly broken. We're lucky he passed out."

"We have to move him out of this rain. I'll get a blanket," Adam said. When he came back, he had a blanket, a flask of brandy, and an axe at his waist. At Will's questioning eyebrow, he said, "I need to cut splits."

The viscount's approving look warmed him.

"I'm not completely worthless," he muttered.

"Not even slightly," Will retorted.

The two of them rolled Avram onto the blanket, carried

him to a sheltered spot beneath an outcrop under Dan's post, and began to set his broken leg.

Adam was tying the last of the strips to hold the splints in place before Avram came around.

"Easy friend," Will said. "He brushed the young man's hair back, raised his head, and offered a sip of brandy.

The patient took it gratefully. "Am I going to die?" Avram groaned.

"Not if we can help it," Adam told him.

"Of course not," Will added. "You need to get back to that beautiful Hebrew scholar waiting for you in Mont-Ombre."

A faint smile from Avram rewarded that statement. "But the gold. You'll have to leave me here. I can't hold you up. I—"

Will silenced him with another sip of brandy.

"We can't leave him here," Will told Adam when the two men slumped down, backs to the rock under the overhang. "We will have to go back down and start over."

"If we do that, you'll be weeks getting home," Adam replied.

Both men sat in silent thought for a while, each lost in regret at the delay.

"We could leave one of the boys with him," Adam suggested, "but we'd have to leave a musket."

"And load all the gold into the other two wagons. If we're going to do that, we may as well send them back down to Mont-Ombre. With one of the muskets."

More silent contemplation as rain poured down and the other three men struggled to unload the recalcitrant wagon. Neither had a better idea.

"My lord, Mr. Halevy!"

Dan's whisper from above them sounded frantic. Adam swung out of the shelter and looked where the young man pointed. A troop of soldiers had materialized out of the rain and mist—five, no eight. A patrol. In these hills, it could be either army.

"Hold fire," Will reminded them, squinting intently into the clearing. "Let's see who they are and what they—Jamie!" He roared and charged down the hill, leaping along and side-stepping rocks.

The leader of the patrol jumped off his horse and ran to meet the viscount. Watching the two men embrace, Adam muttered, "Well, I guess they are friendly," and started down the hill.

"You're two days late. We decided to come farther this way in case you had problems," the major Will called Jamie said, taking in the stuck wagon, the mud, and the bedraggled workers.

"I won't pretend I'm not glad to see you even if you will remind me of this day for the next twenty years."

When Adam approached, Will didn't hesitate. "Major James Heyworth, may I present Mr. Adam Halevy, my partner in this enterprise. Adam, this is the Honorable James—"

The major put out his hand to shake before Adam could so much as bow his head. *Honorable? Another one?*

"Jamie!" the major said, shaking Adam's hand. "No room for the honorable nonsense out here." He turned to his troops. "Well, you lazy slackers, let's get this wagon out of the goo and get busy helping Old Hooky make payroll."

The transfer of gold took over an hour and turning the wagons another. By nightfall, gold had been stowed in the saddles and bags of a dozen horses, Avram had been loaded onto a bed of straw, and all three wagons were on their way downhill, Dan with a musket over his knees. The chickens that couldn't be tied to soldiers' saddle horns for stew pots had been sent home with with the wagons.

Adam glanced at Will riding beside him several days later.

November passed well into December, the chickens had all given their lives for soldiers' dinners, and still the journey continued. They had divided into two patrols, Adam traveling with the one called Jamie, and Will leading the other. When they had reunited just that morning, the delight the sight of his partner gave him stunned Adam. He had missed him.

"How many days do you think it will take us to get back?" he asked.

"Too long. Even with no load and assuming we talk Wellington out of faster horses—maybe half the time, but still too long," Will answered sadly.

"I'm sorry you'll miss your holidays."

"And you already did, no?" The viscount looked sympathetic. They rode for a while, and then he went on. "Will Miss Baumann attend the Duchess of Haverford's charity ball?"

"Probably." Almost certainly. "Baumann will see to it."

"They'll be there until the new year," Will mused. "You might—"

A sudden quickening among the troops distracted them. The major stood in his stirrups ten yards in front and shouted, "Do you do want a good hot meal and shelter or not? Headquarters is around that rise."

Wellington himself thanked them for delivering the prize intact, but the great man had little patience and no time for niceties. They found themselves summarily dismissed with properly signed receipts for the War Office and Baumann's bank. The great man stopped at the door and turned to look at Will. "Did not expect to find you here again, Rochlin. Did Smithson give you your message?" The door shut behind him.

It took them twenty minutes to track down Colonel Smithson. "Hard journey out there, eh?" the colonel said, rifling through piles on his desk. "Friends in the War Office, Rochlin? Message from Glenaire, of all people. Best not ignore that one, eh?" He pulled up a heavy vellum message, its impressive seals broken. The colonel didn't apologize. "Your father has taken a turn for the worse. Glenaire's yacht has been at the coast a week already. It'll get you home soonest. Best not tarry."

After one night in a warm bed, and a good meal, they were on their way through friendly territory with fast horses and a light guard who waved them on their way before sun dipped very far in the sky.

"You'll make it home on time," Adam said as they climbed aboard the yacht.

"Perhaps," the viscount answered, accepting the captain's greeting. "Wind and tide permitting."

Adam hoped it would be so for the man he now thought of as friend. For himself, he hoped only for the shortest route possible to Esther Baumann.

CHAPTER 6

Aunt Dinah complained when she stepped out of the carriage. "That step is too low." She snarled at the footman, "Careful there! Don't break my fingers. Hold me firmly so I don't fall." Then she stepped down on the uneven pavement, groaned, and grabbed the young man's arm.

The contradictory complaints made Esther's stomach lurch. Her aunt's fussing almost ruined her arrival at Hollystone Hall. Almost. Nothing could squelch Esther's wonder at the long causeway through magical water gardens or at the building's glorious façade with its banks of mullioned windows. The air, crisp and clear, filled her lungs. A girl—no, a woman, she reminded herself—who lived in London all her days had no idea how wondrous country air felt on the skin.

Esther had caught sight of massive bushes, thick with berries, from which the hall took its name on the drive in, and thought of her mother's tiny patch of garden in Bishopsgate. Perhaps fresh air and well-tended plants might be the greatest luxury of all; city child that she was, she had never considered the idea.

There was little time to ponder or to enjoy the grounds because a squad of servants flowed down of the massive front steps while the stern face of Saunders, the Hollystone butler, urged them to efficient efforts. Reba rescued Esther's small bag before it disappeared up the steps along with her aunt's sewing basket and the bulkier luggage being unloaded in lively fashion. Esther found herself swept along into the cavernous foyer of the hall with Reba right behind her.

Ladies do not run. Ladies do not skip. Ladies walk with grace. She wanted to dance, but she knew ladies would not do that upon entering a home either.

"Her Grace apologizes for not greeting you herself," an older woman said. "I am Mrs. Saunders, the housekeeper. Her Grace has been detained. She hopes to join you and the other guests in the gold drawing room after you've had a moment to freshen up. Maud will show you to your room." A graceful hand gesture called forward a young girl, who bobbed a shallow curtsey. Esther suspected the girl must be the youngest, smallest maid.

"Oh thank goodness." Aunt Dinah sighed. "Travel wearies one so. Kindly give my regrets to Her Grace regarding this evening. I have blessedly brought my headache powders and will keep to my bed. Please see that tea is sent up,"

If Aunt Dinah worried Mrs. Saunders, the housekeeper didn't show it. She whispered a command to a footman, who disappeared into the house, probably to respond to Aunt Dinah's demands. The aunt glared pointedly at Esther until her niece moved to follow the maid up the sweeping staircase. Esther looked longingly over her shoulder but didn't linger.

The sunny guest room astonished Esther with its simple but beautiful furniture, luxurious bed hangings, and, most wonderful of all, windows overlooking Hollystone Hall's sweeping front drive. In short order, Esther's cloak and bonnet had been stored, hot water for washing arrived, and Reba began to unpack. Esther felt torn between standing in the window, lost in the view, and hurrying downstairs.

Through the connecting door, she could hear Aunt Dinah harangue Maud, whose services she claimed for her own. Esther opened the door, shot Maud a sympathetic look, and spoke to her aunt. "I believe I'll go down, Aunt. Her Grace seems to expect it." She bit the inside of her lip and prayed her aunt didn't want her to dance attendance.

"Go, go then. Leave me to my misery. This one will do." Aunt Dinah gestured toward Maud with a languid hand. "And shut that door. Your room has too much light."

Esther did as she was asked but stood looking at the closed door. Reba paused in her work long enough to smile. "Go then. I'll make sure little Maud comes to no harm. Good luck to you and remember—"

"—behave as a lady at all times."

"I was going to say, 'You're as good as any of them,' but yes. Remember."

Esther took a few steps down the hallway and paused to remember the way. She suspected Maud had been assigned to make sure she knew the way, but she didn't want to open her aunt's door another time. Relief settled on her when she spied a footman carrying hot water jugs to another guest down the corridor. He couldn't stop to guide her, but his directions sounded clear enough.

It took Esther thirty minutes to reach the appointed drawing room. Something caught her eye at every step. She paused to study paintings along the halls, to appreciate the glorious wooden paneling on the first floor landing, and to run her hand along the polished banister. While servants bustled up and down the servants' stairs, the main staircase and entrance hall were empty for now and she could look her fill. A bookcase at the top of the stairs surprised her. A close inspection showed it to be full of novels, poetry, and travel books, the sort of things a guest might want to borrow for an evening's read before sleep.

The grandfather clock in the entrance hall pleased her. It appeared to be almost as fine as the one she delighted in at her father's house. She examined it when an outburst of laughter reminded her of her destination. The sound of conversation drew her toward a door opened merely an inch, in front of which a footman stood ready to admit her. The others, she realized, had arrived the day before, while she and Aunt Dinah took their Sabbath rest at coaching inn.

One voice rang out over the drone of conversation. "Has the little Jewish girl arrived yet? One is curious to meet a Hebrew chit."

Another outburst of tittering giggles greeted that statement.

The man's voice went on, "I don't know whether to expect her face to be coarse or her manners. Do you suppose her skin is dusky?"

The words forced her to take a step backward. The footman, who had leaned to open the door, straightened and looked at her curiously. "Ma'am?"

Before Esther could act on her impulse to retreat upstairs, Reba's words held her in place. *You're as good as any of them.* She pulled herself up, smoothed her skirts, and raised her chin before nodding at the footman.

He sent her a cheeky grin. "In you go then," he said. He, at least, looked friendly.

Esther prayed she would find one familiar face on the other side of the door, someone she knew from school or Miss Clemens's Oxford Street Book Palace and Tea Rooms who could introduce her. The door opened, and she took several steps inside before conversation stopped.

"Ah, Esther, you've arrived! I'm so glad."

The Duchess of Haverford's voice behind her pulled Esther's heart up from the depths where it had settled. She turned and sank into a deep curtsey.

The duchess took both her hands. "My, but you look lovely for one who traveled so far today! Let me introduce you." Before Esther could react the duchess led her arm in arm around the room. The introductions made her head spin. Lady Elinor Lacey looked kind enough and she remembered Miss Vanessa Sedgley from the house-party committee. She barely remembered some of the other names.

When they stopped in front of a man whose open stare passed all bounds of courtesy, Esther knew she beheld the owner of the disembodied voice she had heard. Face to face, he appeared more insensitive than cruel, more curious than amused at her expense.

"Miss Esther Baumann, may I present Mr. Wesley Winderfield, " the duchess said.

Mr. Winderfield bowed quite properly and looked at her with dancing eyes. "Enchanted," he sighed, "Completely enchanted. I am your undying servant."

Winderfield, the annoying man, clung to her side to her dismay and followed while the duchess continued her introductions, ending with some blessedly familiar faces.

"Of course I know Miss Baumann quite well, Your Grace!" Lady Sophia Belvoir said. "Felicity will be delighted to see you, Esther. She has been quite anxious to ask you questions about Hollystone Hall's art collection." The older girl smiled at the duchess. "She didn't want to pester Her Grace with questions."

"Miss Baumann knows art?" the little man gushed. "How marvelous. A savant in our very midst." The fool sounded amazed as though he discovered a dog could walk on its hind legs.

Esther bit back a rude retort. Her father often had cause

to deal in art in the course of his business, either because he received fine pieces as collateral or simply because they made sound investment. Their home displayed many of these works, some permanently. He had encouraged her interest and seen to her education by fellows of the Royal Academy.

"What think you of that one, Miss Baumann?" Wesley Winderfield asked, indicating a large round painting, Raphael's Madonna della Sedia.

It was a copy of course, but as Esther examined it closely, a very good one, possibly sixteenth century. "It looks almost contemporary to the original!" she exclaimed.

"What do you mean, Miss Baumann?" Winderfield asked, looking askance at his hostess. "Do you mean to imply this painting is not an original?"

"It certainly is not." The Duchess of Haverford chuckled. "Miss Baumann is quite correct."

"A copy yes, but an excellent one," Esther murmured, "and quite valuable. I applaud your good fortune to own such a piece, Your Grace."

"I refuse to let Lady Felicity Belvoir drag you into a weary discussion about art. Some of us plan card games. Do you play, Miss Baumann?" Winderfield asked.

Esther would rather explore Hollystone's treasures with her friend Felicity, but she had no polite way to refuse to take Winderfield's arm. She just hoped he really was as harmless as he appeared.

CHAPTER 7

The Weasel—as Felicity urged her to call Wesley Winderfield—flirted through the afternoon and the sumptuous buffet the same evening. For a few days, he hovered at Esther's side. His charm, ridiculous as it sometimes appeared, drew others to her side, but no particular gentlemen sought her out. That suited Esther.

The second day, she paused before the door to the breakfast room, bit her lip, and hoped. Surely, it is too early for the Weasel. When the footman opened the door, she scanned the room, and her heart soared. Felicity Belvoir had arrived before her as they had planned, and—joy of joys—she saw no sign of the Weasel.

Two steps in, she saw a man turn from the buffet and almost tripped. Felicity was not alone after all! The Earl of Hythe, looking like the perfection of English manhood in his fashionable coat and perfectly tied neckcloth smiled at her. Her eyes flickered over his perfectly groomed hair, handsome face, and… She swallowed at the sight of his form and well-fitted trousers and felt heat slip up her neck. The earl laid his plate on the table and inclined his head toward her.

"Miss Baumann," he said in greeting.

Esther bowed deeply and felt her hands shake when the earl held out her chair and asked what she preferred to eat.

"Coddled eggs and toast will do, my lord, and thank you," she replied, breathless at the thought of an earl serving her breakfast.

The amiable young man proved as easy to talk to as his sisters, however, so much so she found herself confiding that she found the Weasel's attention somewhat confining.

"I can see where he might have that impact on a lady." Hythe chuckled. "You may be spared today. He will sleep until noon after—" The earl hesitated, and Esther suspected that he believed ladies ought to be spared whatever the Weasel, and for that matter the other gentlemen, had been up to the night before. He cleared his throat. "He has agreed to take a part in a billiards tournament this afternoon."

"Yes, but this evening…"

"The hunt ball? Never fear, Miss Baumann, I'll rescue you if he crowds in again." He smiled warmly, and she found herself growing more comfortable.

When he offered to escort Esther and his sister on their planned tour of the house, she discovered that she liked him very much. The three began their quest in the Hall's gallery and then wandered out into passages and stairways covered with fine pieces. The collection made Esther yearn to see what the Grenfords, the Duke of Haverford's family, had at their primary seat or London home.

The earl demonstrated the sort of general knowledge of art that any well-educated man—at least one who paid attention—might have. Between them, the earl and Esther gave Felicity a primer on styles and artists. He didn't talk down to Esther and never contradicted her observations, but it wasn't until he mentioned one particular bronze that she realized he actually respected her expertise.

"It sits nestled in a window alcove on the third floor of the guest wing," he told her, leading them in that direction. "It looks Roman to me, but I wondered what you might think."

He led her to a sunny alcove with windows on three sides. A marble pedestal about waist high had been placed in the alcove, and a small bronze statue sat on it. She might have known it would be a horse. What else would draw a gentleman's attention?

"What do you think, Miss Baumann?" the lord asked, rocking back on the balls of his feet like an excited schoolboy.

Her hands itched to touch the object. She clutched them behind her back to avoid temptation and leaned over it, moving her head every which way to see it from every angle.

"So is it Roman?" he demanded.

"Greek, actually, or perhaps both. Or perhaps a copy."

"Can't you tell?"

"For certain? No. If it is fake, it is exquisitely done." She stood upright to look at him. "The Romans were master copiers, turning out many fine reproductions of Greek work."

"Hence both."

"Or neither. It's difficult to tell."

"But you quickly identified the Raphael as a copy."

Esther brushed his words aside. "The whereabouts of the original Raphael are well known. Besides, paintings are easier." She looked back at the lovely little piece. "I do know one thing. Whoever did this had great skill. If it is a copy, it wasn't done by a hack."

The earl nodded gravely, lost in thought.

"You have an eye for quality," Esther told him.

"Not as much as you do," he said with a grin.

He'll make some woman an agreeable husband.

The earl noted that the sun had come out and, if they bundled up warmly, they might take a turn around the gardens.

The poor man must have had his fill of my babbling. "Take your sister out for some air, my lord," she said. "It's time I checked on my Aunt Dinah." She watched them go and breathed deeply, needing a moment to calm herself.

She hadn't lied about her aunt. Esther found the woman sitting up in a frilly bed jacket, sipping her chocolate. "Dressed and up I see," she said. "What have you done that is useful?"

Esther bit back a smile when she remembered just how long she had been "dressed and up."

"I toured the house with my friend Felicity and her brother," she told the old woman.

"You went walking with a young man!" Aunt Dinah interrupted. She chewed her lower lip. "I suppose his sister lent you countenance, but you must be cautious, Esther. Young men are not to be trusted. They are, are . . . a hazard to young women." She punctuated that odd statement with a sharp nod. "Who is this man? Is he anyone?"

"He is the Earl of Hythe."

"An earl! Oh my. Yes. Goodness. That's all right then. The sister accompanied you. Must be acceptable." Aunt Dinah took another drink of chocolate and picked up a book in pink binding with flowers embossed in the cover, obviously satisfied that she had done her duty as a chaperone. She waved Esther on with a flick of her hand.

Esther turned to leave, but something moving under her aunt's coverlet caught her eye.

"What is that!" she asked, but her aunt pretended not to notice. She lifted a corner, and a small gray head appeared. Black eyes blinked at her. Esther jumped back, and the kitten, gray from ears to the tip of its tail, leaped down and ran out the open door.

Aunt Dinah kept her eyes in her book, but Esther wasn't fooled, especially when she noticed a saucer of cream just inside the door. She shook her head and crossed to her own room.

Reba proved less encouraging. "A sister is well enough, Esther, but don't go wandering down those passages alone with a man. A lady—"

Esther made a wry face. "I know what a lady would and would not do, Reba."

Why hadn't she gone with her friends? Why hadn't she jumped at the chance for a turn around the gardens with the handsome earl? Every other girl at the party would have.

"He is *goyim*, girl—not a Jew. Nothing will come of it," Reba went on without looking at her.

Does she think I want to marry every man I speak to? I don't, even one as pleasant as Hythe.

Before her restlessness could overtake her, a footman knocked at the door, and Reba brought over a message.

"Sophie and Felicity are making plans with some of the others," she told her companion. "They invited me to join them."

"What plans?"

"They don't say. I'll be back to dress for dinner, if not before," she said with a smile, and skipped out before the older woman could lecture her further.

She found the sisters and Miss Cedrica Grenford, who twirled a feathery quill in her hands and seemed intent on making a point.

"We're deciding on costumes for the masquerade," Felicity told her in lieu of greeting.

Esther sat with a thump. "Masquerade? Aren't those scandalous?"

"Dear me no," Miss Grenford said. "Not in the Duchess of Haverford's household."

Sophia raised an eyebrow and pursed her lips as if she might make a sharp retort. She did not. "They don't need to be. Miss Grenford suggests we use it as an opportunity to demonstrate an interest in English history. It's to take place on the evening after Boxing Day." Her lips twitched as if she suppressed a smile, but Sophia Belvoir would never be so unkind as to mock another.

"Improving subject or no, I fear the available costumes may limit us to the English kings and queens," Felicity said, gesturing toward the jumble of boxes and trunks against one wall, "although I make no doubt Lady Miranda will come as some sort of pagan goddess."

"Felicity, really! You don't know that!" Sophia said with a reproving look. "And you'll shock Miss Grenford."

"What do you have so far?" Esther asked.

"Sophia claimed Elizabeth already," Felicity moaned. "I am trying to decide between Anne Boleyn and Mary Queen of Scots."

"Who else do you have on your list?" Esther asked.

Miss Grenford raised the hand with the quill and scanned down the paper. "How about Mary of Modena? You have an exotic air and could pull it off."

Exotic air? Does she mean not English enough? "The woman who caused James II to be deposed? I think not," she said out loud. Queens don't get much more non-English than that.

Determined to find a solid English name, she pulled the paper away from the woman and looked the list over.

One name struck her. She walked over and rummaged through the boxes, pulling out a gown of silver lace over gray underskirt and giving it a shake. "Can this be given a Tudor look?" she asked, holding it at arm's length to look it over.

41

"The sleeves are certainly wide enough," Sophia mused. "I think it might work if we flatten the front and add a white fichu to raise the neckline. We'll all need board fronts if we're to come as Tudors. Who do you have in mind?"

Esther pulled the gown across her front, holding it in place at the waist with one hand and at shoulders with the other. "Lady Jane Grey, of course," she said with grin. "Or at least Lady Jane in gray."

"Perfect!" Felicity exclaimed. "I think I'll do Anne Boleyn. I could tie a red ribbon around my neck. Wouldn't that be famous?"

"Gruesome, rather," Miss Grenford said with a shudder.

"If we want to convince Hythe to be Henry VIII, that might be a bit awkward," Sophia pointed out.

"Ugh. It would make me your mother, too. I think not. Mary Queen of Scots it shall be. I can still wear the red ribbon."

"Will he do it? Your brother seems like a good sport," Esther said over laughter. She folded the silver gown over one arm.

"Do you like him?" Felicity asked, eyes dancing.

"Felicity!" Sophia exclaimed.

"Oh my goodness," Miss Grenford gasped at exactly the same time.

Esther felt her cheeks burn. She swallowed hard. "I haven't met a Belvoir who was anything but charming. His lordship's conversation this morning proved delightful."

Sophia nodded her approval. "If I might risk being as forward as my sister, Esther, did you find my brother attractive?"

"Any woman would! His face and—" Esther stopped and bit her lower lip. "Yes."

"He's very young," Sophia said in a warning tone.

"I can see that. You needn't fear I have designs on your

brother. If he helps me avoid the Weasel, I shall be grateful to him however."

Sophia watched her shrewdly. "I suspect, dear Esther, that the truth is your heart is already engaged elsewhere."

Esther hadn't thought it possible to color any more brightly, but the heat creeping up her neck made her doubt it.

"Is it someone here?" Felicity demanded.

Esther stared at her tightly clasped hands, aware of the Belvoir ladies' scrutiny. "There might be, but he would never come here. Perhaps there would be someone if I found a man who respected learning as much as a well-run household."

Before Felicity could press for more, Sophia murmured, "Just so."

CHAPTER 8

Wind and tides in their favor, Rochlin and Adam reached London at dawn on December twenty-fourth and dashed up the stairs of the War Department sooner than either dared hope to deliver receipts, reports, and gratitude to Glenaire. Adam left them then, the two friends to make their grim errand to Chadbourn Hall and he to deliver one final report.

Nathaniel Baumann looked on his protégé with astonishment. "I expected two more weeks at least! Come, come, sit. You look exhausted—and none too tidy, let me say." The older man viewed the receipts with satisfaction. His obvious relief surprised Adam. The man rarely showed doubt or insecurity. "Found the man himself, I see, and delivered every crown and pence. Good, good," Baumann said, rubbing his hands. "How did you find Rebbe Nahmany?"

"As wise and shrewd as ever. Happy to strike a blow to the Corsican."

"And the War Office?"

"Satisfied. More than satisfied. Glenaire sends his personal thanks." Baumann appeared pleased at that, but

Adam leaned forward before the older man could launch into further discussion. "Is Miss Baumann in?" he asked.

The banker sank against the back of his chair, brows raised. "My Esther?" His lips twitched. "Hundreds of miles through hostile territory into a war zone, sharp doings with the War Department, and your first concern is to ask after Esther?"

Adam squeezed his eyes shut. Not well done. He had thought of little else for days.

"My daughter is a guest of the Duchess of Haverford at Hollystone Hall this week, Halevy. Is there something you wish to discuss with me?"

"You let her go?" Adam exclaimed, eyes wide.

Baumann made his face stern with apparent effort. Adam might have worried but . . . The old man has a twinkle in his eye. That bodes well, doesn't it?

"My daughter has very influential and gracious friends. The event is for a good cause. Why would I not allow her to attend?" Baumann leaned forward confidentially. "She has her aunt to lend her countenance, and I have had assurance from Her Grace that the proposed Jewish Free School will receive some support."

Astounding. Adam wondered how the rabbis would react to that support. Before he could ask, another implication hit him. "Does Esther know the school is intended for boys only?"

His employer looked discomforted. "She should," he said. He waved a hand as if to dismiss the matter. "Change will come with time."

Adam had no time to debate issues, religious or secular. Esther is at Hollystone in any case, probably absorbing the duchess's well-known progressive views. He shook off disappointment. "It is Esther—Miss Baumann—I wish to discuss."

Baumann's amusement broke into the open. "I thought

you might. What is it you want?"

Two hours later, Adam left in the Baumann's carriage. He refused shelter for the night, changed to another set of clothes only slightly less rumpled from travel than the ones he wore, packed the best he had, and agreed to several conditions, one of which he planned to ignore. He would go through the motions of accepting a matchmaker's services only after he knew Esther's heart. If she would not have him, he would not force tradition on her.

Hollystone lay one long day by carriage from London or at most a day and a half. Adam planned, insofar as he thought it through rationally, to travel through the day in spite of his late start, to change horses, travel through the night on the main road, and to arrive the following morning. He forgot the rest of the world celebrated Christmas; he forgot he lacked an invitation; and he forgot to consider the roads made soft by days of rain and crowded with holiday travelers. The pace of the Baumann carriage, lurching slowly along rutted and pitted roads, gave him ample time to reconsider.

By the time the sun dipped low on the horizon and a posting inn loomed ahead glowing in the orange light of sunset, Adam had had enough.

"Two horses, Sir?" the innkeeper whined. "I be hard pressed to find you one good saddle horse." Behind him, the sound of drunken revelry and ribald songs filled the air. "I kin offer you a good meal tonight an' a feast to break your fast tomorra', but you may have to sleep in th' taproom."

A wise man would take the offer. After a good night's sleep, the horses would be rested. He could make Hollystone by nightfall barring a broken axel or mired wheel. He glanced toward the taproom. Hollystone Hall's revels would surely be more refined, but he wondered what sort of English customs Esther would be part of. Worse. What sort of English gentlemen has she met? He would go on.

∼

STANDING on the brick pavement in front of the solid stone walls of the Haverford Orphan Asylum, Esther listened to her friends and fellow guests serenade the young inmates with Christmas carols but did not join in, much though she admired them. She wondered if anyone serenaded the inmates of the Jewish orphanage in London on their holy days and felt a frisson of guilt. Her parents were patrons of the place, but she had visited it only once. When she watched Her Grace distribute little gifts, pat heads, and inquire about each child's wellbeing, she realized how important personal touch was to those poor unfortunates and vowed to do better.

"I could teach you the words," a voice hissed in her ear. The Weasel sidled up to her. Many of the gentlemen, Hythe included, had found reasons to be elsewhere, but the Weasel had happily announced he would, "Protect the ladies. Have 'em almost to myself, don't you know."

She forced a smile. "I know many of them, Mr. Winderfield for I've heard them often, but they aren't my songs."

He looked momentarily taken aback. "Why, they are everyone's—but, of course! Not your tradition. I see. Do your people have Christmas songs, Miss Baumann?"

Esther narrowly avoided rolling her eyes. "We have music for all our holy days," she replied.

"Holy days." The Weasel chuckled. "Different ones, right? Stands to reason. Clever that." He winged an arm. "Her Grace is ready to return to the Hall. May I?"

She took his arm, hiding her reluctance. *Honestly, Esther, the man is harmless. Merely foolish.* Foolish and insensitive.

The Weasel kept up a steady stream of chatter that required little of Esther other than nods and the occasional, "Why, yes, it was exciting." The hunt. Lord Tipton's victory at billiards. Miss Cedrica Grenford's victory at charades. It didn't matter. He seemed more enthralled with his own commentary than Esther's reaction.

"I say, did you hear?" he asked at last, bending toward her.

Esther sent a swift prayer of hope that he hadn't realized her inattention or noticed her heating face. "I apologize Mr. Winderfield I missed what you said."

"I asked what you planned for tomorrow. Not going to the church service I'll warrant."

"No. I'll attend my aunt while the rest you go off to Saint Agnes in the Holly. We plan some quiet time. Perhaps we'll peruse some improving tracts."

"I say, do Hebrew girls get those horrid tracts as well? My cousins loathe the things."

Luckily Hollystone Hall loomed in front of them, their fellow guests let out a cheer, and no response seemed necessary. Esther turned her bonnet and cloak over to Reba who met her in the front entrance, suddenly missing her mother more than she might have credited a week before. At Reba's frown of concern, she managed a wan smile.

A disturbance in the hall and murmurs of interest from the guests caught her attention, however. "Unexpected guest." "Uninvited more like." Other comments in speculative tones were unintelligible.

Uninvited guest? A surge of hope almost upended Esther. Has Adam come? Did he have a change of heart? She tamped down her foolish thoughts. Adam was in France. Adam didn't approve of house parties.

"Good gad, m'cousin's come!" the Weasel exclaimed.

As high as her heart had soared, so it sank low. Esther took dejected steps up the stairs, determined to seek some solitude. She said a swift prayer for Adam asking the almighty to keep him safe, wherever he might be.

CHAPTER 9

S leeping rough had become second nature to Adam, but when the lowing of sheep behind a low stone wall woke him up cold and hungry on Christmas morning, he vowed never to do it again. He had ridden almost to the door of the Hall in the wee hours of night before common sense led him to withdraw. Bad enough to arrive uninvited; worse to awaken the household hours before dawn.

He rolled to sit, groaned, and put his head on his knees. Light stretched along the horizon at the end of the road. A few more hours loomed before he might present himself at the Hall. Two horses cropped the weeds where he had left them the night before. He rummaged in his bags for the stale, but filling, bread his erstwhile innkeeper grudgingly supplied along with the horses, one a decent hack and the other a reluctant carriage horse pressed into service primarily to carry his bags. The carriage nag had briefly served to relieve the other but had been skittish when saddled.

It took him an hour to locate a stream, and moments to

wash. Adam briefly considered changing his clothing but gave it up as a hopeless case. Glancing at the sky, he shook his head. Still too early. Would the household be at breakfast? His stomach rumbled at the thought. No. I'll wait another hour.

His bound Torah with rabbinical commentary in the margins served him well and a stump made a perfect seat on which to read. His mind went unerringly to Beginnings.

> Isaac brought her into the tent of his mother Sarah, and he married Rebekah. So she became his wife, and he loved her; and Isaac was comforted.

Isaac was comforted. He smiled at that and remembered Sarah Nahmany. Could Esther read this passage? Or the other… a man shall cling to his wife… Suddenly he wanted her to know Hebrew and the commentaries, too. Wanted it for her sake. When she was his wife he would see to it. The thought warmed him while he waited for the sun to rise higher.

～

ESTHER SUSPECTED Aunt Dinah ignored every word she read, but there seemed little to do but go on. The household had breakfasted early and gone to services. Surely they will be back soon. She sighed and continued reading.

"Pardon the interruption, Miss Baumann. There's a… The footman's hesitation seemed to rise from puzzlement. "… gentleman to see you. Shall I tell him you are not in? Ordinarily I wouldn't hesitate to deny him, but after the uproar yesterday, and Mr. Saunders said…"

Clearly the unusual comings and goings had rattled the duchess's staff. Esther heard over her morning coffee that both of the Duchess of Haverford's sons had arrived quite late in the evening, causing almost as much of an uproar as the Weasel's notorious cousin.

"Did this gentleman leave a calling card?" Aunt Dinah sniffed. She had made her opinions of uninvited guests clear the night before.

"No, ma'am. He said to tell Miss Baumann he came directly from France and had no time to—"

Esther shot to her feet, the book forgotten in a heap at her feet. Her throat ached at the pounding of her heart.

"Perhaps it is Viscount Rochlin. He was invited, was he not?" Aunt Dinah said in dampening tones.

Esther stared over the footman's shoulder through the open door.

Aunt Dinah gave a weary sigh. "There is one way to find out," the old woman declared. "Show him in, but remain at hand please."

The lanky form of Adam Halevy filled the doorway. The room seemed to shrink around him when he came forward to greet Aunt Dinah properly, though his eyes never left Esther who stood, stunned, in front of her chair.

"Miss Baumann, my apologies for arriving unannounced. Your father informed me of your whereabouts and I...I, ah, had to come and see about your welfare," he finished lamely.

My welfare? The words shook Esther from her shock at the sight of him. *My welfare? Why would I need a keeper? I'm under the duchess's hospitality.* All her resentment rushed back.

"I am well, as you can see," she snapped. "I am a guest of this house, enjoying the duchess's hospitality as you—" are not...

"Mr. Halevy! Mr. Saunders informed me of your arrival. I am so sorry I wasn't here to greet you." The Duchess of

Haverford swept into the room, her cheeks rosy from the trip back from church, looked at the two young people, and quickly assessed the situation. "I understand you have a missive for me?"

Adam bowed low. "Your Grace. I apologize for the intrusion." Though his obeisance was entirely proper, Esther thought his travel dirt and dishevelment ruined the effect. What must Her Grace think?

Adam retrieved a thick vellum packet from his coat. When Her Grace slit the wax and flipped it open, Esther recognized her father's characteristic seal and dramatic handwriting.

The duchess broke into a warm smile. "I'm delighted you have decided to contribute to our charity ball and even more delighted that you've arrived on time to assist with our holiday revels. I'll certainly make you welcome as Mr. Baumann urges, but I fear accommodations are in short supply. You may imagine we are full to the rafters."

"I apologize for the inconvenience, Your Grace. I'll sleep over the stable if that would help. I don't require much."

"Nonsense, young man! We do not put guests in the stable. Viscount Elfingham also arrived late. He took our last guest room, but he won't mind sharing. I'm certain of it." She looked him up and down shrewdly and murmured, "Yes, I think the two of you will get on nicely." She rose, her warm smile encompassing both Esther and Adam. "Now I'm sure you will want to clean up before you come to spend some time with our Miss Esther."

When Cedrica Grenford entered, the duchess introduced the woman as her protégée. "She will show you up. You'll find today's itinerary in the room. Viscount Elfingham will be pleased to make your acquaintance. He could use an ally."

If that last remark piqued Adam's curiosity, he showed no

sign. He followed Cedrica. What else could he do? She watched him go, torn between relief and frustration. *Why has he come? And why does the duchess think the Weasel's cousin needs an ally?*

CHAPTER 10

For one moment, regrettably brief, Adam saw joy in Esther's face at his arrival. Her eyes lit up when she saw him, but the shutter went down too soon, and she got her back up. He had no idea why expressing concern for her welfare made her dig in her heels, but it had. He suspected he might have to grovel. *Does anyone understand women?* he wondered, following the quiet young woman the duchess had introduced. *I don't.* Perhaps a decent suit of clothing and a shave would help.

She showed him to a modest-sized bedroom dominated by a massive and quite wide four-poster bed, before taking her leave discreetly. *There will be room enough for two at least,* he thought wryly. *But I hope there aren't more latecomers.*

A gentleman stood with his hands behind his back, looking out the window, and he turned at Adam's arrival. His dark complexion and exotic air told Adam all he needed to know about Her Grace's cryptic remark about allies. Adam wondered if anyone had told him he would have a roommate.

The viscount seemed merely curious, if his raised brow was any indication.

Adam straightened up and bowed. "My lord, I am Adam Halevy. I regret to tell you Her Grace has assigned me to share your room. I apologize for any inconvenience."

A warm smile lit Elfingham's face. "No reason for regret. We latecomers must be grateful for any welcome at all." He put out a hand. "Elfingham—James Winderfield. Pleased to make your acquaintance, Halevy."

Adam shook his hand, relieved the man didn't seem to mind. *How will he feel when he knows I'm a Jew?* Rochlin didn't mind. Perhaps this one won't either.

A discreet clearing of throat drew Adam's attention, as did some commotion. His baggage had arrived. "If I may, Mr. Halevy, I will see to it your clothing is pressed and returned to you. If you have some to be laundered, may it wait until tomorrow? Her Grace gives servants some time for themselves on Christmas," the young footman who brought it said earnestly.

Adam thanked him and requested hot water for shaving. The footman promised it would arrive but said, "We being that short today, and you with no valet, it may be some time before I can return to shave you."

"Not needed. I manage to shave myself daily."

The servant withdrew, looking absurdly grateful.

"They do like to make us helpless, don't they?" Elfingham said. "As if a man can't see to his own needs."

Adam counted that notion in the viscount's favor. He took a good look at the man he would be forced to share space with for a week. Tall and dark, the viscount gave the impression of coiled strength. His manners put Adam quickly at his ease, particularly after Adam laid his Torah with its Hebrew titles on the shared desk and Elfingham did not so much as raise an eyebrow.

Sometime later, Adam paused at the door behind which the buzz of conversation rose and fell. He would socialize. He got on easily with Elfingham, and he counted Rochlin a friend. Perhaps he could even find Esther's comfort with English society, if not her joy. He would even celebrate their holy day if he had to. But he would talk to Esther alone as soon as he could manage it and lay his heart open. He could only hope she might do the same.

≈

ESTHER FLOATED through the afternoon in shock. She could think of only one reason Adam had come. *Papa sent him to check on me.* She was not about to give the arrogant man the time of day and put her efforts into staying away from him.

Cards, music, and quiet occupations filled the afternoon, and Esther managed to sidestep Adam at every turn. For once she had been grateful for the Weasel, who danced attendance and managed to avoid completely insulting Adam when he realized Adam was Jewish as well.

The one time she found herself alone, he began to walk toward her. She spun around to Cedrica Grenford and begged her to come upstairs to check a tear in her hem. There was, of course, no problem with her gown.

When she returned to the drawing room, tea had been delivered and people sat in small groups around the room, enjoying the bounty of the house. Her restless gaze found Adam standing with the Belvoir ladies and their brother. He smiled down at Felicity Belvoir, who looked utterly rapt.

Esther knew she should move. All afternoon she had avoided him, but at that moment, she could not make her feet move. *What has Felicity so fascinated? Is he telling her about Spain? Did he actually meet Wellington? What of his perilous journey?* Longing to know kept her fixed in place even as her stubbornness urged her to move away before someone noticed she stared. Too late! Hythe glanced up, saw her, and smiled.

Hythe bowed over her hand and said, "Your friend has had quite an epic adventure."

"Is that what he's telling Felicity?" she asked with a haughty shake of her head.

Hythe's lips twitched, and she felt her cheeks heat. When he offered his arm, panic set in. *Does he mean to walk me back to his sisters? Adam is there, the wretch!*

Hythe followed the direction of her eyes. "Shall we take a turn about the room, Miss Baumann?" he asked. When she laid a shaking hand on his and nodded, he patted her it with his gloved one, changed the topic of conversation to riding mishaps at the hunt, and soon had her laughing.

An hour later, Esther, relieved to have passed the afternoon without being cornered, she felt composed and less shaken. *If Mr. Halevy wishes to speak with me, I'll permit it. It is foolish to allow him to discomfort me. I'll be all that is cool and in control.*

When she spied him across the room speaking with one of the Duke of Ashbury's daughters, he looked at her across the expanse of room and smiled with such sweetness that her heart skipped two beats, her composure fled, and her toe caught on the rug. Esther might have stumbled had not a gentleman caught her elbow before she fell. She looked up at a tall gentleman with piercing eyes and a swarthy complexion. The Weasel's cousin. How could two men be more different? she wondered, even as she thanked him graciously.

Before he could reply, or Esther could decide whether or not to let Adam approach, the Duchess of Haverford rose at the end of the room and rang an ornate silver bell for attention.

"Indulge me before we go up to dress for dinner," Her

Grace began. "By happy coincidence, today is not only Christmas, but very shortly, it will also be the beginning of the Jewish Sabbath." She gestured toward a window through which the sun could clearly be seen dipping below the horizon. "As you know, this time is sacred to some of our guests. Since they have been gracious enough to share our celebration, it behooves us to share theirs, no?" She raised a hand in a graceful gesture, and liveried servant wheeled a teacart with silver candlesticks, a decanter of wine, and a loaf of bread laid out upon it.

The duchess spoke directly to Adam, who stood several feet away. "Mr. Halevy, would you be so kind as to lead us in your blessing?"

Adam looked back with an inscrutable expression. Esther feared he would refuse. *Can he bear to be singled out this way?* She glanced frantically around the room, fearing she might see disdain. She found none, except perhaps on Lady Stanton's perpetually sour expression. She appeared to grumble to someone beside her. For the rest, Esther saw nothing but interest. *Can Adam feel their good will?*

He bowed before the duchess moments later. "I would be happy to oblige you, Your Grace, but it is customarily the lady of the house who says the Sabbath blessing. Might I suggest instead that Miss Baumann lead us?" He turned and looked directly at Esther.

Every eye in the room followed his, and her heart dropped to her belly. Felicity clapped her hands; Cedrica Grenford smiled approvingly; the Weasel seemed merely curious. Hythe's habitual expression of good cheer restored her composure.

"Well, my dear?" the duchess asked.

Esther forced her feet forward and curtseyed. "Of course, Your Grace. It would be my honor." She stepped to the teacart, made sure all was in place, and pulled her shawl, all silvery lace, up over her head before she smiled around the room at large. "For the sake of the company, I'll use English, I think."

Her hands didn't shake when she lit the candles or when she waved them over the flames with infinite care once, twice, three times. She covered her face with steady fingers and prayed silently for a moment. Then she raised her voice:

"Blessed are you, Lord, our God, sovereign of the universe

Who has sanctified us with His commandments and commanded us

To light the lights of Shabbat."

"Amen." She heard Adam murmur it quietly but firmly and lowered her hands, opening them to look down on the Sabbath lights, memories of home, her grandmother, and other Sabbaths filling her.

"Is that all?" Weasel whispered, avid eyes darting between Esther and Adam.

"Not exactly. At home, we might walk to services now and do Kiddush later, but, since we're staying here, that blessing comes next," Adam said, stepping up next to Esther. He poured wine from the decanter into an exquisite crystal goblet etched with a vine and grape pattern. He held it up in front of him. "And there was evening, and there was morning, a sixth day," he began. Esther focused on his long fingers wrapped around the goblet and the sound of his voice "...and he rested on the seventh... and he sanctified it...because it is the first day... Blessed are You, who sanctifies Shabbat," he finished.

Esther said, "Amen," into the hush that followed. He

looked at her then, and for one brief moment, there was just the two of them and Sabbath peace.

It was Sophia who broke the spell. "Lovely," she murmured. "Lovely. Am I right that this is a home ritual, a family service?"

"It is indeed," Adam replied. "Family is at the heart of everything."

~

ADAM WATCHED Sophia Belvoir introduce Esther to Lord Jonathon Grenford, the three of them laughing together before the Earl of Hythe offered Esther his escort in to dinner. Adam knew the Grenford brothers' reputations made them inappropriate companions for his Esther. Surely Esther wouldn't be seduced by false charm and the Haverford estate? Of course not. At least it isn't the older Grenford brother. He didn't know Hythe, but he saw the way she smiled at the earl, and he didn't like it one bit.

Seated far from her, he had no opportunity to talk to her, not that dinner would have allowed him to press his case. When the ladies left them to their port—miserable custom that it was—he had no polite way to pursue her.

Grenford's older brother, the Marquis of Aldridge, as ranking male family member, presided over the distribution of cigars, which Adam declined, and port, which he gladly accepted. Aldridge urged the gentlemen to move toward the head of the table for ease of conversation. Talk drifted over horses, hunts, and mills that held no interest for Adam. When the talk turned to politics and the conduct of the war, however, the marquis leaned forward.

"But you were there recently, Halevy, were you not?" Aldridge asked, taking him off guard.

The mission had not been widely known, but neither was

its secrecy vital. Still, he couldn't imagine how Aldridge knew. His surprise must have shown.

"A mission for the War Department, was it not? I had drinks with Glenaire earlier this month, and he mentioned that he had dispatched you with Rochlin. Of course, he kept the details obscure enough."

"Tight as a clam is, Glenaire. You'll get naught from the man," someone complained jovially. "What was it? Ferrying Wellington's private bootblack to the old man?"

Aldridge exchanged a knowing look with Adam.

"Something like that," Adam said. "The marquess was kind enough to send his private yacht to bring us home."

"You were in Spain!" Lord Jonathon Grenford exclaimed. "Tell us everything: the roads, the dangers—the women."

"The drink?" Adam retorted. "You can't fault the French for their wine."

"You went through France?"

"An advantage of being a native speaker," Adam told him. A few stories about bad inns and good food seemed to satisfy, and the conversation moved on.

When they rose to leave, Wesley Winderfield gave Hythe's shoulder a punch. "Henry the Eighth! No fair. Now I'll have to come up with a better king. Perhaps Richard the Third. Shall I limp?"

"Kings?" Adam asked.

"For the costume ball night after next. The Haverford attics lend themselves to kings and queens," Hythe replied. "Who do you favor?"

"You mean I'm expected to dress up and prance around as an English king?" Down the table, he caught Elfingham's eyes.

The viscount's expression gave little away, but Adam doubted the man would make himself one of the Henrys or Edwards, not with his dark eyes and exotic looks.

Adam shook his head as they moved toward the door. "Not my cup of tea, gentlemen."

"But you must! The ladies expect it. Wait until they go to work on you. Wear a man down," Weasel Winderfield grumbled. He didn't wait for a reply.

Aldridge clapped Adam on the back. "Take heart, Halevy. A mask will do." The marquis winked and went on his way.

Did Esther expect him to dress as an English king? If so she would be sorely disappointed. It was asking too much.

CHAPTER 11

A book makes poor company in a house full of people, but Adam could think of no other way to pass the afternoon.

The morning after Christmas, he joined the ladies on their trek to deliver Boxing Day charity, using the Sabbath as his excuse to avoid hunting with the gentlemen. It was true enough, but his chief reason had been the opportunity to corner his quarry. Esther managed to avoid him, even on the return walk, by attaching herself to the Belvoir ladies like a limpet and refusing to meet his eyes. After they returned, she had disappeared into the upper floors.

I can hardly pursue her to her bedroom, tempting though that thought is. With every day that passed, her father's arrival came closer, and he had to speak to her first. If Baumann arrived, matchmaker in tow, without warning, she would feel trapped. She would refuse him in some humiliating fashion or accept him because she saw no way out. He determined to avoid both at all cost, but he couldn't pursue her.

Books it is. When he entered Hollystone's massive library, however, he wasn't alone.

"Hiding, Elfingham?"

The lord looked up over his book, rolled his eyes, and said, "Not hiding. Licking my wounds more like."

"Shooting birds doesn't appeal?" Adam teased.

"I've taken down much more challenging game but not as challenging as my current quarry."

"Lady Sophia?"

Elfingham closed his book. "She avoids me at every turn. You?"

"Giving the poor birds a rest, and yes, I'm not having success either. Ladies can be damned elusive in a pile as massive as this one."

The viscount smiled. "It's bigger than some villages in Turkestan. I thought a house party would give me the opportunity I needed, but no."

Adam nodded sympathetically. He explained Baumann's plans and his concern. "I have two days to press my case and at least give her a choice. It's damned hard to court a woman who won't even speak with you."

Humor shone from the viscount's eyes, "You may have to overcome some of your gentlemanly instincts, Halevy."

"She deserves better. I'd rather keep it above board—and dignified."

Elfingham raised a questioning brow.

"The costume ball. I don't see me prancing along next to your cousin in tights."

"They want to force us into some sort of English mold," the viscount agreed. "It won't fit. They see me as a wild Turkmen prince. I plan to give them one."

The man's quiet confidence filled Adam with envy. "Well done, you! I wish I had your choices. Somehow, I don't think a village rabbi will have the same impact."

"Perhaps your Esther would prefer a Persian King."

Adam didn't take his meaning at first. When it dawned, he gasped and his mind exploded with ideas. "Ahasuerus!"

"As the Bible calls him, or Xerxes. Your objection isn't to all costumes, I take it then, merely to foolish ones?"

"The king and Esther… it would be perfect, but I doubt that the Haverford attics will lend themselves to such a costume."

"Perhaps not entirely but I have some things that may help. We could manage it quite nicely."

"You would do that for me, Elfingham? I'm grateful."

"James, please, if we're to be co-conspirators." He put out a hand to shake. "May I call you Adam?"

Adam took the man's hand. "Happily, James. The women won't be able to ignore us tomorrow night at least."

"That they will not," said James with a lupine gleam in his eyes. "That they will not."

∾

WHEN SHE STARTED WANDERING the halls midmorning, Esther told herself—and anyone who stopped to chat—that she wanted to take another tour of the fine art. In her heart, she knew better. For once, Adam ignored her, and she felt perversely curious about his whereabouts. He had gone off with Viscount Elfingham right after breakfast, and she found herself looking for him around every corner. *At least he isn't pursuing a lady. As if I would care!*

She couldn't imagine what captured the two gentlemen's attention. Neither seemed the sort to avoid the rest of the guests, even to escape Lady Stanton's overt bigotry, Weasel's idiocy, and some of the others' fawning delight in "our exotic fellow guests." Hythe obviously bore Elfingham some offense, but he had been perfectly amiable to Adam, as had the Grenfords and many of the others.

Both appeared at luncheon looking smug and pleased with themselves. Both followed some of the other gentlemen to the billiard room with every show of enthusiasm. She almost followed, but Felicity dragooned her into making final adjustments to their costumes.

The day dragged on, and when Adam appeared at tea only to spend a half hour chatting about politics with the Marquis of Aldridge, she had a hard time keeping her eyes away from the two of them.

"The marquis is lovely to look at," Felicity moaned, "but entirely ineligible. A lady's reputation is at risk merely being caught in conversation."

Esther murmured polite agreement. It wasn't the marquis who interested her.

Lord Jonathon Grenford joined their conversation. He insisted she call him Gren because, "everyone does."

"I understand you are an art expert," he said with a teasing glint in his eyes.

"Hardly! But I've had cause to learn," she replied, enjoying his flirting.

"Would you care for a stroll through the garden? The sun has blessed us this afternoon. A warm shawl might just do."

Felicity had left them to speak to Cedrica. Did she dare? She took his offered arm and allowed him to lead her out of the French doors under his mother's pointed gaze. She hoped Adam saw them but didn't dare look back.

"I believe he watched," Gren said. "In fact, I'm sure of it."

Heat reached Esther's brows. "I don't know what you mean," she said primly.

"Don't you just?" Gren grinned. "Halevy misses nothing that you do."

"That's because my father sent him to spy on me."

Gren's bark of laughter startled the sparrows. "Come

now, Miss Baumann. I don't believe you are so innocent that you don't understand the look in his eyes."

She frowned at the young man's words. *Even if Adam wants me, he is disagreeable and, and—* She couldn't think what.

"Let's give him cause to worry, shall we?" he asked, tugging her toward the hedges.

She giggled when he pulled her by the hand and dashed for the stables once they were out of sight of the windows. In the gloom of the barn, he led her directly to a stall near the back.

"Ah, there they are. Visiting Mama, are you?" he asked. Five—no six—kittens of various colors wrestled in the straw while their snow-white mother looked on.

"Goodness! The one who haunts my aunt's room is all gray. That one is tiger striped, and the one next to him is black. Do they have multiple mothers?"

"Multiple fathers more like." Gren reached down to pick one up. "Cats have no morals."

Like some men, she thought. *Not Adam though. He will be a steadfast husband and always there when his wife needs him. Whoever she might be, some poor girl who lets a man run her life.*

When they returned, he was gone, and he didn't return when supper, a light repast since the costume ball loomed, was served.

Neither the giggling girls nor even Lady Sophia's determined cheer distracted her when she followed them all upstairs to dress for the ball. Why couldn't Adam be as obliging as Hythe? She wondered if he would appear at the ball in so much as a mask, or even if he would attend it at all.

CHAPTER 12

Lady Jane Grey may not have been an inspired choice. Esther's notion to dress entirely in gray from slippers to headdress had proven to be depressing. The dress, though lovely, faded into the background next to the colorful gowns of the others. She had briefly considered snatching the gray kitten from Aunt Dinah's room and tucking him in her sleeve but took pity on him in the end. The kitten might have helped.

Sophia looked glorious if somewhat stiff in her Elizabethan costume. Esther could tell her friend was distracted, however. She seemed to be scanning the room nervously exactly as Esther herself was doing.

Cedrica Grenford stunned in a shepherdess costume. Esther should never have listened to her business about English history as an improving activity.

Weasel limped around saying, "Richard the third don't you know," to anyone who would listen. His hump teetered back and forth as he walked.

There were knights in unimpressive armor, a friar, and

some milkmaids who looked less than respectable. She saw the duchess escort one from the room.

Two gentlemen in formal dress leaned gracefully against an ornate mantelpiece at one end of the ballroom. Each wore a simple mask, one black and one white; neither wore a costume. Could one be Adam? Esther inched her way in that direction. She had not gone very far however when she realized her mistake. There could be no denying Aldridge's confident posture and arrogant tilt of head. Is the one next to him Gren? The incorrigible flirt confirmed it with a wink and a cocky salute. At least he noticed her.

A young lady rather scantily clad as a Greek goddess, Lady Miranda, she suspected, swooped in front of the brothers and drew their complete attention. Even at a distance, she could see them both shift into the role of charming rake, no costume needed. She pressed her lips together to suppress her amusement at their transparency. *Adam would never do that.* The thought came unbidden. She wasn't sure it was welcome. *Where is the wretch anyway?*

She continued her circuit of the room and found a few other gentlemen who opted for the simple mask. None were Adam. It would be just like him to turn up his nose at a costume ball and not even bother to wear a mask.

A disturbance across the room caught her attention. Ladies fluttered around someone, obviously taken with a man's costume. Curiosity kept her watching until the group shifted, parting so Esther had a good look. The man wore a costume of some sort of eastern potentate.

"What's this then," the Weasel asked loudly. "Some Egyptian pharaoh?"

Esther couldn't hear the man's reply, but he turned his gaze her direction, and she forgot to breathe.

"Persian king? You ain't my half breed cousin. Who are you?" the Weasel demanded.

She heard the reply this time.

"Ahasuerus," the man said, looking directly at her.

Ahasuerus. The Persian king who chose a Jewish bride and loved her enough to help her people. A Jewish bride. Esther.

Lights danced in front of her eyes, and for a moment, Esther thought she might faint. She gripped a waist-high urn full of ferns as the man walked toward her and made a deep bow. Whispers flowed in waves around the room, and though she didn't listen with her ears, Esther's heart knew they concerned her and the story of the king.

"Will you walk with me, my lady?" the man asked in a familiar voice.

Adam's voice. He had come.

When she put her hand in his, he held it high in a courtly manner and began to promenade around the room, nodding as a gracious king might do to the curious and amused onlookers. He promenaded past the grinning Grenford brothers, Hythe in his Tudor tights, and the duchess dressed as Catherine the Great. He promenaded past the entire company and walked her out the door, down the hall, and into a small withdrawing room. Esther moved along beside him, stunned into inaction.

Before she could register that he had closed them in alone, he tore the false beard from his face—wincing a bit when the adhesive stuck to his skin—tossed it aside, and took her in his arms with a predatory gleam in his eyes. She couldn't move while his mouth descended toward hers. She wondered distantly if she ought to refuse his kiss, but no power on earth could make her do so. The moment she had dreamed about, longed for, and denied since the moment he came to work for her father three years before had arrived.

She leaned into it, and curiosity gave way to wonder. His mouth felt warm and firm against hers. He began to move, and warmth filled her too, fire bursting forth deep inside her. Then his tongue touched her lips, and her knees gave so that he had to pull her against his body until they touched, shoulder to knees, and she thought she might melt. What could she do? She responded in kind, tongue to tongue, and gripped him in return.

They both were panting when he pulled his mouth away and cradled her head against his shoulder. "Will you listen to me now, Esther?"

~

ADAM TRIED to gather his scattered thoughts from the fog of lust. Her response had been much more than he dared hope. He set her firmly on her feet and slid his hands down her arms, putting a few inches between them.

"We need to talk." But how to start? Her deep brown eyes boring into his didn't help. He kissed her again.

When she groaned against his mouth, he put her away from him and walked toward a shuttered window on the other side of the room. "When you look at me that way, I can't think," he said.

"You think too much," Esther replied with a sly smile, stepping toward him.

He let his head drop back. "I need to tell you I was wrong. It isn't easy for me."

She stopped and rocked back on her heels, eyes wide.

He let it all out in a rush: Rochlin's friendship, Sarah's Hebrew, and Rebbe Nahmany's advice. "'Keep an open heart,'" he said. "I didn't understand what he meant at first, but he was right. You were right. I need to trust, to give people and ideas a chance."

"Ideas?" she murmured. She looked baffled by his jumbled words.

71

"We can value our traditions without becoming so hidebound we can't allow change. We can hold on to our own customs and still value our friends."

She scrunched up her face in an adorable expression as though she was hard at work sorting his words. "What was it you said about Sarah Nahmany?" she asked.

"She reads Hebrew. Her father has begun to teach her, alongside her brothers and—"

Esther's expression stopped him. She almost glowed in wonder. "Would you teach me, Adam?" she whispered.

"Yes. And our daughters, too." She was in his arms before he could add, "If we have any," before he could ask her to marry him, before he could warn her about her father's plans. The intensity of her response almost shredded his last self-control. It might have, if the sound of scuffling and laughter outside the door hadn't startled both of them.

They leaped apart, Esther with one hand to her lips, Adam still holding the other. The intruders moved on.

"We have to go back. They'll all wonder—I'll be a disgrace," Esther exclaimed, sinking to her knees and looking for the remnants of his costume beard. She rose with most of it in a triumphant gesture.

His opportunity had passed. He helped her restore her hair where it had come loose from her headdress and cupped the side of her face. "You go, Esther. I'll stay here for a while so we don't go back together, but we must talk. Will you come for a walk with me in the morning?"

She punctuated her agreement with a swift kiss on his lips and left in a flurry of skirts. He crushed the false beard in his hand. The costume had done its work. He had no desire to wear it again and less to face the revelers or watch Esther dancing and flirting.

He would see her in the morning.

CHAPTER 13

The sunlight shimmering across the carpet looked as bright as Esther felt. She was bursting with impatience while Reba helped her dress.

"Hold still," the maid said. "Stop dancing around the room if you want me to get this done." She tied the ribbon around Esther's bodice in the back and gave it a pat. "There. A lovely bow."

Esther danced away and made a pirouette.

"Miss Esther! Your mother says—"

"This morning I don't care, Reba!" Esther went to the window, leaning on the sill to look out over the lane. "Isn't it glor—"

"What is it, Miss Esther?"

"Papa," she whispered, staring out the window. "What is he doing here?"

Far below, the familiar figure of her father stepped out of the Baumann carriage. Footman swarmed around to help, but he turned back to the carriage and handed down another passenger. Even from her second floor room, Esther could see it was not her mother. Mama wasn't well enough to travel in any case.

The woman, stout and past middle age, wore an unfashionable bonnet and colorless clothing. Esther recognized her at once from temple as one of those widows active in charity, active in community events, and active in everyone's business. The matchmaker. Her heart sank. Papa had made a match for her. She watched the carriage with eyes so sharp her head hurt, but no one else emerged.

She turned and marched into Aunt Dinah's room. The woman lay in a bed jacket, sipping chocolate, the gray kitten curled up next to her.

"Did you know my father planned to come?" Esther demanded.

Aunt Dinah blinked back. "What? No? What has gotten in to you? Nathaniel is here?"

"He brought the matchmaker," Esther said sourly.

"Good. It is time he made a match for you."

"I don't… That is, I hoped… Oh!" She stamped her foot in frustration and left the old woman to her chocolate.

A pounding on her door made her cringe. "Is Papa demanding to see me already?" she moaned.

Reba went to the door and reared back in outrage. "Mr. Halevy, you cannot come in here! It isn't proper."

"Esther," Adam called over the maid's shoulder. "Your father is here. I have to talk to you." He went around Reba and took Esther by the hand. "He's early."

"You knew he planned to come," she accused, pulling her hand away in outrage.

"Yes, but I thought I had another day or two."

"What do you mean?" Outrage gave way to puzzlement.

"Esther, I need to know if you want me. The matchmaker will put the question. If you're going to reject me, I'd rather if you do it now. I won't let you be forced into something you don't want," he said fiercely.

"You won't?" she murmured. Puzzlement gave way to hope.

"Of course not. These aren't the middle ages, and I'll not have a wife who was forced to do something she doesn't want," he replied, stiffening. "What you must think of me!"

Her naughty thoughts about him did not bear saying out loud. Joy bubbled up from deep inside. "Wife, Adam?"

"What do you think I was trying to tell you last night?"

"As I recall, there wasn't lot of talking involved," she replied, growing warm at the memory.

He ran a frustrated hand through his hair. "I'm making a mess of this. Will you marry me, Esther? I can't promise we won't quarrel, but I'll do my best to listen to you."

"To keep an open heart?"

At the sweetness of his smile, she almost capitulated. "Yes, that," he said.

He reached for her then, but she put out a hand to stop him. Hope had given way to joy, yet she needed to hear the words.

"But why? Why do you want to marry me?"

"Why? Being near you drives me mad. I love you, Esther. That has to count for something."

"Oh, yes," she said, closing the distance between them. "It counts for everything."

"Miss Esther! What would your mother say? A lady—"

Esther lost herself in Adam's kiss. For once, she didn't care what a lady might do.

THEY FACED HER FATHER TOGETHER. From the force with

which Esther gripped his hand, Adam knew she felt less confident than she pretended.

Baumann had been shown into the breakfast room along with Mrs. Lipson, the matchmaker, who sat fanning herself and looking rather like a bedraggled sheepdog.

Baumann stiffened at the sight of them. "You're making free with my daughter's hand, Halevy. She isn't yours yet," the old man said to the amusement of several young ladies who watched them avidly.

"I was just suggesting to Mr. Baumann that business might best be conducted after a good breakfast," the Marquis of Aldridge drawled, saluting Adam with his coffee from his seat at the head of the table.

"An excellent suggestion, my lord," Esther said primly. "Mr. Halevy, would you kindly obtain a plate for me?"

She gave her father a swift peck on the cheek and took a seat far from Mrs. Lipson. Unfortunately that put her next to Aldridge and brought a frown from her father. Adam didn't like her sitting next to London's most notorious rake much either.

"Do you plan to break your fast, Papa, or have you already done so? And tell me how you came to arrive so early in the morning."

Baumann sat next to his daughter. "We stayed at the Rose and Rooster last night. We had a bit to eat there," he said, accepting coffee from a footman.

From the way Mrs. Lipson tucked into coddled eggs and kippers, it must have be a small bit.

Adam watched his love manage her father, who was obviously torn between amusement and concern. *No doubt she will manage me as well.* He looked forward to it.

She hadn't told him what she wanted to eat, so he gave her a bit of everything. When they married, he would learn her likes and dislikes. He smiled to himself and took a seat next to Aldridge. The humor lurking behind the marquis's attempt at a bland expression face sent his appetite to perdition. He settled for coffee.

"How did you leave Mama?" Esther asked. Adam suspected another question *why did you leave her* lurked beneath her words.

"Worried about you," her father answered, glancing over at Aldridge. "Of course your Aunt Dinah is here. Where is Dinah?"

"Taking chocolate in her room. She has enjoyed her stay," she answered sweetly before peppering him for gossip, asking after his painful knee and tossing in some shockingly shrewd business questions.

Baumann murmured replies until he reached his limit and pushed himself up. "Enough, Esther. I need to speak to you," he pinned Adam with a look, "and Mr. Halevy, if the marquis would be so kind as to direct us to a private room."

"We will need witnesses," Mrs. Lipson piped up from the other end of the table, waving a spoon in the air. "Best call Dinah down."

"A moment, if you please, Baumann," Aldridge said, rising. "Perhaps while we wait for Miss Dinah Baumann to be summoned?" He gestured to a footman and sent him after Esther's aunt.

Adam glanced over at Esther when her father and the marquis stepped out into the hall. She merely shrugged as if to say she had no idea what business they might have. Aldridge then leaned in and said something that seemed to please Baumann.

The men sipped their coffee until a servant entered and whispered something to Aldridge. The marquis looked at Esther and, seemingly satisfied with what he saw, suggested they follow him to a room arranged for her father's purposes.

Esther looked more confident than Adam felt when he helped her rise. Baumann glared at him until he dropped his hand from her waist and offered his arm properly. They all waited while the matchmaker put both hands on the table and pushed her bulk up, muttering irritable remarks about failure to "do it properly" and young people in general. Esther smiled up at him; they would be as proper as the occasion required, as long as he got what his heart demanded in the end.

CHAPTER 14

Someone who didn't know Adam might see a young man overflowing with confidence. Esther knew better. She could feel the tension in his arm and see it in the tight smile he gave her. He probably thought she needed reassurance. Dear sweet idiot.

When they followed Aldridge into a second floor sitting room, Aunt Dinah fluttered in one corner in diaphanous shawls, but the woman in the center of the room would have reassured Esther things would go well, if she weren't already perfectly certain she could manage Papa. The Duchess of Haverford took both Esther's hands in hers, examined Esther carefully, and smiled warmly. "I'm to wish you happy?" she asked.

Esther nodded, a lump in her throat making speech impossible for a moment.

After much bowing and greetings, Mrs. Lipson clapped her hands. The woman knew her business. All eyes looked her way.

"Miss Esther Baumann, it is my pleasure to announce that

your father has arranged a most advantageous marriage for you to a fine Jewish man of excellent family."

Esther looked up at Adam standing next to her with narrowed eyes. He shrugged. Of course he spoke to Papa first. She couldn't hold that against him.

"I assume you agree to this match."

"Yes," Esther murmured.

It seemed to be enough. The matchmaker went on without waiting. "Mr. Halevy, I assume you will agree to a traditional *ketubah* with amounts agreed to between you and Mr. Baumann."

"Wait!" Esther exclaimed. She frowned. "Traditional? May I see the wording?"

"What is a *ketubah*?" the duchess asked.

"It's a marriage contract," Adam explained, "for a woman's protection. The husband agrees to provide her with food, shelter, and—" He colored and looked around the room.

"—and her marital pleasure," the matchmaker finished, "as is a wife's right." She gave a firm nod.

"Quite so," Adam said. The look he gave Esther almost melted her toes. He would have no trouble fulfilling that obligation. Esther's imagination ran away with her, momentarily distracting her from the question.

"A contract to protect wives," the duchess declared, "How enlightened."

"A promise of pleasure," Aldridge murmured. "Very enlightened."

"And he agrees to a sum put aside for her should he put her aside or die before her," the matchmaker explained.

"Like marriage settlements?" Aldridge asked.

"Exactly like marriage settlements," Adam said.

"But not, I suspect, enforceable in law."

"No. Secular legal settlements will be required." Baumann said. "Halevy and I have yet to negotiate the details."

The blasted men talked about Esther's future as if she wasn't there. That snapped her out of her distraction.

"I want to see the wording," she demanded, "of the *ketubah* and the settlements."

All three men turned to look at her with astonishment. Her father looked outraged, Aldridge amused, and Adam? She couldn't decipher his expression. It was almost as if he was frustrated that he had missed a particularly important point in his studies.

"The wording is traditional," the matchmaker said, pulling a rolled up paper from her sleeve, "although some men feel the need to add clauses. I don't approve."

Esther took it from her. "This isn't Hebrew," she said.

"Aramaic," Adam said, looking over her shoulder. "Legal language. Shall I read it?"

She handed it over with a glare.

"Shall I teach you Aramaic, too?" he asked with a smile that almost chased her annoyance away.

"That's it?" she asked when he finished. "You'll provide a house, feed my children, and, um, otherwise care for me? Can we add to it?"

"No," the matchmaker said.

"Yes," Adam said at the same time. "What would you add?"

"I want to add that all our daughters will be educated as well as our sons," she said, raising her chin.

That statement provoked a strangled noise from her father and applause from the duchess.

"What nonsense!" Aunt Dinah and the matchmaker exclaimed simultaneously.

"I agree," Adam said at the same time. Their eyes caught, and for a moment, the others might as well have been in the Antipodes.

"It also says you will pay 200 pieces of silver to buy me," she whispered, still staring into his eyes.

He blinked and ran a hand across the back of his neck. "The silver is traditional, and it isn't for purchase! The money is put in escrow for your protection in case something happens to me. The amount is negotiable."

"The settlements?"

He nodded.

"Very well. You and my father may draw up the first draft of settlements, but I want to review them before you sign— and I want an English translation of the *ketubah* as well. If I like what I see, I'll marry you."

Against a background of gasps and a few chuckles, Adam drew back at first, but then he smiled and leaned forward until their foreheads touched. "You will like what you see, or I'll make it right. I promise."

~

IN THE END it took two days, particularly after Esther pointed out a nasty loophole regarding control of their daughters' dowries, before Aldridge sent to London for their family solicitor. By December thirtieth, the settlement draft was complete.

Adam worked at a desk in his room, translating the *ketubah* into English—the traditional passages in which he agreed to protect and provide for his wife, assure her of her rights to the marriage bed, and insure her sustenance he added "and educate her sons and daughters in the faith of our fathers."

He included the sum he agreed to as his portion of the more complex settlements and stared down at it for several moments. Baumann's contribution dwarfed his. He picked up the pen and added "and to protect her dowry with all due care." Let Mrs. Lipson make of that what she will.

He looked over at the clock on the chest of drawers. They

had agreed to meet in the gold drawing room at ten. The duchess seemed determined to make an event of what would normally be a private event. There had been a brief uproar over the date of the wedding when the duchess suggested they wed on the day of her ball by special license, but, of course, Jews didn't use special license. They were exempt from the Hardwicke Act, and their own law and custom required at least a thirty-day period between the agreement and the marriage.

Baumann and Esther already argued about the wait, with his love asking for a date as soon as they could arrange a wedding and Baumann insisting it would take months to arrange "a proper wedding," by which he meant one that would turn London on its ear. Adam could only hope she won out, but he suspected Baumann would be ruthless in getting his own way.

As it was, he had hardly seen Esther in two days and certainly had not had any opportunity to get her alone. Her father chaperoned her tightly, and even her aunt woke up enough to keep her protected.

With the translation in his pocket, he detoured toward the rooms of the lady guests and lurked on the landing, hope in his heart. Her footsteps alerted him when she left her room, and a quick look down the hall assured him of privacy. She jumped when he snaked an arm out to pull her close but quickly wrapped her own arms around him and returned his kiss.

"I've needed that." He sighed.

"Aunt Dinah's on her way," Esther warned. "We only have a minute."

"I wanted to tell you I'm leaving as soon as the settlements are signed."

"You aren't staying for the ball?" She frowned.

"They'll only allow me a dance or two if I stay, and,

Esther, I'm not sure I can be nearby and not be able to touch you," he explained. She looked smug at that, his not-so-innocent darling. "Besides, I need to find a house. I promised to shelter you, remember?"

The sound of a door made them take a step apart, and he offered his arm properly as Aunt Dinah approached.

Their fellow guests packed the drawing room. As he surmised, the duchess had outdone herself. Champagne on ice and trays of wine flutes were at the ready along with iced cakes. He had no doubt Baumann planned a formal—and lengthy—blessing for the occasion. An inlaid mahogany library table had been drawn up in the center of the room with a legal-looking document and an excessively fluffy quill on it. Baumann sat there, tapping his knee impatiently.

"Shall we?" he asked when Adam entered.

Both men signed the settlement papers, to the polite congratulations of the company.

"Wait," Adam said, still seated after his turn to sign. "While not usual, I wish to add something." On the bottom of the settlement, he wrote, "I, Esther Baumann, have seen and agree to this," and prayed the solicitor wouldn't have fits or demand to do it over. He stood held out a hand to Esther, who grinned when he helped her to the chair and handed her the quill.

She signed in a dainty hand and looked up at him, "And the *ketubah*?"

He unrolled the document he had written out in English under the curious eyes of their non-Jewish friends and began to read it. Esther listened as intently as the others. At "and daughters," he heard a whispered, "Bravo!" from Sophia Belvoir.

"It is our custom to sign this contract at the wedding, and it is necessary that the formal copy be in Aramaic," Adam explained. "I'll ask a calligrapher to create a beautiful document for Esther, one she can display in our home. However, for the sake of this company, with all of you as witnesses, I would like to suggest Esther and I sign this English copy as a pledge of our love."

Esther looked up at him, stunned, tears pooling in her eyes. Had he miss-stepped? She looked down at the translation he had given her, quill poised in one hand, and didn't move. He waited, holding his breath. The entire crowd around them waited. Her father looked like an explosion was building.

I did everything I could think of! What more does she want? He couldn't stand it any longer. He took the quill from her hand and pulled her to her feet.

"Excuse me," he said to the room at large. "Esther and I need to talk." Before anyone could stop him, he had her out the door, down the hall, and into a small alcove.

"What do—" he began.

Esther stopped him with her lips, standing on tiptoe and weeping tears into his mouth. "It is beautiful, Adam, perfect," she said between kisses.

He didn't pretend to understand women, but he took full advantage, deepening the kiss until they were both breathless and panting. He pulled away and leaned his forehead on hers. "Are you going to marry me, Esther?"

"Of course! What do you think, you nodcock?"

"Then sign the blasted paper, so everyone knows it."

Her mouth tilted in wide smile. "Anything you say, Adam. I plan to be a very submissive wife."

He chuckled. "I doubt it, love, but luckily, I have a very open heart."

ABOUT THE AUTHOR

About Caroline Warfield

Traveler, would-be adventurer, librarian, technology manager—Caroline Warfield has been many things, but above all she has always been a romantic. Now she writes historical romance. Enamored of owls, books, history, and beautiful gardens, she sits in an office surrounded by windows while her characters lead her to adventures in England and the far flung corners of the British Empire, and she nudges them to explore the riskiest territory of all, the human heart.

Website: http://www.carolinewarfield.com/
Facebook https://www.facebook.com/carolinewarfield7
Twitter: https://twitter.com/CaroWarfield
Pinterest: https://www.pinterest.com/warfieldcaro/

OTHER BOOKS BY CAROLINE WARFIELD

Dangerous Works

A little Greek is one thing; the art of love is another. Only Andrew ever tried to teach Lady Georgiana both.

Dangerous Secrets

Jamie will do anything, even enter a sham marriage with his employer, to protect a little child. Will love—and the truth—bind them both together?

Dangerous Weakness

The marquess will chase her as far as he needs to—even into pirate-infested waters—to protect her. Can he win her love as well?

A Dangerous Nativity

With Christmas coming, can the Earl of Chadbourn repair a damaged estate and a far more damaged family? Will he find love in the bargain?

Children of Empire Series

Three cousins, driven to the far corners of empire by lies and deceit work their way home, uplifted by the women they love.

Book 1: The Renegade Wife

Rand may be a reluctant hero, but he quickly realized Meggy and her children needed protection, Now she's gone again, and time is running out for him to save them all.

Book 2: The Reluctant Wife

Whenever Fred Wheatly tried to do the honorable thing he came out a loser. Now his career in the Bengal Army is in shreds, he has two children to raise, and a stubborn woman keeps pricking his conscience. This time failure is not an option.

Made in the USA
Middletown, DE
15 November 2019

78663570R00057